…N

… in County Durham in 1914 and educated at the Dragon School, Oxford and Wrekin College. He entered the Navy in 1932, retiring in 1946, and his career included service on Earl Mountbatten's staff and a part in the North African, Sicilian and Normandy landings. After the war he was under contract to the late Ted Kavanagh of ITMA fame, writing for radio and television, later becoming concerned with film-making. He has travelled widely, especially in America and eastern Europe. He lives in Surrey.

Apart from plays, film scripts and historical books, he has written eleven other novels, the first having been published in 1950. They include the 'Tarnham' secret service thrillers – *A Matter of Diplomacy*, and *The Tarnham Convention* (to be published in Pan, 1973). His immensely successful novel about Gibraltar, *The Rock* is being reissued simultaneously by Pan.

By the same author in Pan Books

THE ROCK

A MATTER OF DIPLOMACY

THE POWDER TRAIN

WARREN TUTE

UNABRIDGED

PAN BOOKS LTD : LONDON

First published 1970 by J.M. Dent and Sons Ltd.
This edition published 1972 by Pan Books Ltd,
33 Tothill Street, London, SW1.

ISBN 0 330 23254 1

Printed and bound in England by
Hazell Watson & Viney Ltd,
Aylesbury, Bucks

I

Now she was late, thanks to that annoying man from the Czech Embassy. She hurried down the Cornmarket trying to control her impatience and anxiety. In Prague you could keep a boy waiting on a date, she was not at all sure you could do it in Oxford. The streets were thronged on this dry, cold February night and her skin tingled as she slithered through the crowd of undergraduates on her way to the pub which Philip had assigned as their meeting place. She cursed Mr Patoček in her own language for making her late and for reminding her of the grim realities she had for the moment left behind in Czechoslovakia.

'What's the hurry, Anna la Bella?' a familiar epicene voice said as she tore round a corner, 'Won't Philip wait for his pretty Czech chick? He waits for me.'

'Oh! hallo Broyster.' She stopped, fuming at this added delay.

'Brewster,' he corrected her. 'Are you coming along later? The Group will be at Matterlys.'

'It depends on Philip.'

'Well, if lovely Philip wants to connect with our scene he can't do it long distance.'

'I'll tell him.'

'You do that, doll. Tell him it's in his interest to be there around eleven o'clock.'

She smiled at him briefly and sped on her way, wondering if behind it all Brewster was merely trying to make Philip. Or was he a pusher? Philip had once told her that Brewster MacFish – and surely that name wasn't real – had developed a wide range of promotional interests. He sees himself as a latter-day Diaghilev, Philip had said, but really he's just a mini Mafia man. She did not like him at all. Her father would have said he was 'not cultured' though her mother, with her theatrical background, would no doubt have got his true measure in an instant. With an impatient shake of the head, she put Brewster MacFish out of her mind.

The pub in a back street off St Giles was currently where it was at, in the language Anna seemed always to be catching up on. It was the scene at this time of the evening for foreign students visiting Oxford. When she got there it was packed. Philip stood at the far end of the bar, talking to an older man with angry dark eyes and the hard cynical look of the compulsive drinker. They seemed to be arguing and for a moment Anna hesitated to join them. She had had enough emotional disturbance for one evening.

She caught Philip's eye and then darted off to the loo, thinking that by the time she emerged, he would have got rid of the older man. But this didn't work and when eventually she joined them, Philip was in one of his raw petulant states which made her wonder if he wasn't homosexual after all. There was only one way of finding that out and she was not interested enough in their relationship for that experiment. Philip had called her a prude, adding that in his opinion the Czechs were more bourgeois than any suburban student from Surrey but she was not to be taunted into it in that way. She was a solid sexy girl who knew her own mind and even if she did come from an established Communist background she had her own firm set of values so far as men who attracted her were concerned.

'You're very late,' Philip said, 'I was on the point of going.'

'I bumped into Broyster. He says you should come along to Matterlys later on. It would be to your advantage.'

'Brewster can go and chase himself,' Philip said sourly, 'I think that's all he does anyway.'

He bought her a drink but did not introduce the older man. As Philip was paying the barman, the stranger gave Anna an unhurried, concentrated look which made her catch her breath and turn quickly away. The invitation, the knowledge, the experience and the understanding were all there in those disturbing but unaggressive eyes. The balanced pull in the look she received was almost a lazy denial of the invitation itself, as if it didn't matter how she reacted.

'Do you have a cigarette?' she asked Philip.

'Yes, in my right pocket,' Philip said without turning round.

'Here,' said the stranger, pushing across a packet that lay in front of him on the bar. She put her hand across Philip's back to fish out the packet but the other man deftly and firmly took her hand and guided it to the packet on the counter. The touch was complementary to the eyes, firm and yet not in any way grasping, an instant caress.

'Take one of these,' he said, as if there was no question of her doing anything else. The touch had sent a shock through her which she neither wanted nor liked.

'Why don't you keep out of it?' Philip said hotly. 'Anna's with me.'

'What a square, old-fashioned statement!' the stranger said with a sour smile. 'It takes me back to the time I was your age myself.'

He did not press the point but instead withdrew his cigarettes and lit one of them himself with a quick agile gesture, such as a conjurer might have used, which Anna found fascinating in spite of herself. There was no doubt he had a magnetism of which he seemed fully aware, but did not bother to turn on at anything like its possible power.

'Drink up,' Philip said curtly, 'we must be on our way.'

She had no wish to leave as quickly as this, but Philip was in a rage and she was not yet independent enough to make the running herself. When they were outside she allowed her anger to show.

'That was charming!' she said. 'What was all that about? And who was that man?'

'In another few moments he'd have been openly making a pass at you,' Philip said bitterly. 'That was the notorious George Mado – my bastard of a father.'

After Philip and the girl had gone, Mado finished his drink and ordered another double scotch. What makes me do it? he asked himself savagely, why bother? – when every single time you knew what the answer was going to be? He drew on his cigarette and looked round the crowded bar, reacting instinctively to three other mini-skirted undergraduates over by the fire. A lecherous, dirty old man, that's all my son, and no doubt his girl-friend, think me to be. And perhaps that's all I really am, he reflected morosely, at any rate from one point of view.

Almost automatically the training came into play and he got out his notebook while the first impression of her and what he had found out from Philip were still vividly in his mind.

'Annabella Novaček, early twenties, blonde. Slav, blue-grey eyes, five foot ten and at least ten stone, good strong breasts, firm active body, masculine hands, wide nostrils and a sexually capacious mouth.' He almost felt as if he'd just left her bed. 'Reasonably quick-brained and uninhibited. Far more experienced and older in being than the boy she was with' ... my son, he thought, the son who only has time for his mother, who considers his father contemptible trash. He stopped this train of thought abruptly, knowing that it would simply lead to alcoholic depression on a grand scale.

He swallowed his drink in one and immediately ordered the same again. 'Father currently on Czech Trade Mission to the Lebanon. High up in the Party. Possible candidate for the Praesidium. A Novotny man. Mother well-known stage actress. Reputedly a child mistress of one of the *emigré* Hapsburgs. The girl has a pleasant personality, speaks good English and is likely to make student friends during her Oxford semester.'

Instinct made him shut his notebook and put it away a few seconds before a hand fell on his shoulder.

'Hello, Mado!' said an over-oiled voice trying not to be patronizing, 'what brings you to Oxford on a raw February day in the year of our Lord nineteen hundred and sixty-eight?'

Mado attempted to keep the feeling of nausea out of his face without quite succeeding.

'I've been having a drink with my son. How have you escaped from Whitehall?' As if he didn't know. Simon Dinkworthy, old Etonian Whitehall layabout. *Crème de la sour crème*. And with him a sharp little foreigner, all eyes and eagerness.

'Well, officially a board, old boy. Actually I haven't used my expenses for some time so I thought a trip to the city of dreaming spires would just about fill the bill.'

Dinkworthy always talked as if he'd been exposed to an overdose of P. G. Wodehouse in early youth and had never tried too hard to get over it.

'Introduce me to your friend.'

'Ah! yes,' said Dinkworthy in that vague, upper-class way Mado so loathed and detested. 'This is Vladimir Patoček. He's . . . er . . . what did you say you actually did at the Embassy, old boy?'

'I am Assistant Cultural Attaché,' said the Czech proffering his hand and bowing stiffly. 'I'm so glad to meet you so accidentally, Mr Mado.'

Some pleasure, some accident, Mado thought as he stared coldly at the Czech.

'Yes,' he said drily, 'not so many people bother to meet me these days. Let's have a drink.'

By the time they reached the cellar where the Group was playing that night, Anna had begun to pester him with questions. Philip disliked this invasion of privacy and his temper grew steadily worse.

'But if your father's name is Mado, why do you call yourself Philip Carlton?'

'That was Mother's name. When Father left us some ten years ago, we all reverted to Mother's name.'

'Why?'

She found him looking at her with that arrogant impatience young English boys so often had. Philip's eyes were implying that she had no business to probe in this way.

'You don't know my father as we did,' he said coldly.

'He looked rather interesting to me. Sexy at any rate.'

'Well, if that's all you want—'

'It isn't.'

'Anyway you're over the age of consent. He wouldn't be interested in you.'

He then had to explain what the age of consent meant in English law and this made him more irritated than ever.

'Thank God we didn't have the name Mado when it all happened. Mother had enough trouble as it was.'

Mr Patoček had filled in the details for her earlier on but now she played the innocent Czech girl on her first visit to the West.

'When all what happened?'

He looked incredulously at her.

'Surely you heard about the Mado affair in Poland? At the time Father was almost as famous as Greville Wynne but in his case there was no Penkovsky. Father was simply a very ordinary little spy who got caught.'

'So why wasn't he shot?'

'I don't know,' Philip said as if it were painful to him even to remember this train of events. 'I suppose he was more valuable to them alive. They exchanged him later on for one of theirs who got sent down for a thousand years or something, when he hadn't even robbed a train.

I don't know. You ought to be telling me. You're a Communist from a Communist country.'

'I am not. I'm not a member of the Party.'

He looked at her, puzzled.

'Then how did you manage to get to Oxford for a term?'

'My father's a member of the Party. He has influence. Anyway, things are all going to change with Dubček. Didn't you know?'

Brewster MacFish came over, nodded approvingly at Anna, put his arm round Philip's shoulders and kissed the top of his head.

'I've talked to the Group,' he said, 'and they're willing to try you out this weekend. Didcot is the scene, in what used to be a railwaymen's club. They think your voice is OK. Your other abilities need a little attention.'

'Like my guitar-playing, you mean?'

'Like your other qualifications to join the Group need looking at more closely,' said Brewster MacFish, giving Anna the glint of a smile, 'and that, lover boy, falls into my province as the Wanderlust's manager. Rule One is to know just what it is you have to offer when you're stuck up there on that rostrum. The girls only really want what they know they can't have. Anyone will tell you that.' He stood up and touched Philip on the shoulder. 'My place Saturday at five,' he said, and then with another sardonic glance at the girl,' Camp followers make their own transport arrangements.'

After Brewster had left them, they got up and danced. The Wanderlust were blasting away at deafening volume. Both she and Philip danced mechanically, lost in their thoughts. It seemed a million years since she had left Prague. It was even an age since Patoček had reminded her earlier in the evening that she had only been granted an exit visa provided she kept in touch. 'And your boyfriend is of interest to us,' he added as she left.

Later as Philip walked her home through the frosty night, he made an attempt to salvage the evening.

'I'm sorry I was so curt earlier on,' he said, drawing her into an archway and giving her a long, lingering kiss. 'The only trouble with the Wanderlust is that I don't dig Brewster MacFish. Plus seeing my father like that throws me right off track for days. When he shows up unexpectedly like tonight, I always hope it's the last time I'll see him, like will he now leave us alone for ever? But he never does. Maybe I won't see him now for another six months or a year but he always shows up again at the most embarrassing time.'

'I wasn't embarrassed tonight.'

'No, but I was. I always am. I really can't stand the sight of him.'

'What's he do now – for a living?'

'What he always has done, as far as I know. Sells textbooks and tries to flog his services as an educational consultant. He began by running a school in Switzerland for the children of diplomats – I suppose that's how he got into the spying game – but he took too much of the wrong kind of interest in some of his pupils and that came to an abrupt end, with my mother clearing up the mess. Like she always did. Now I think he just sells textbooks and all that. I don't know how well he does. He's for ever travelling abroad.'

'Does he ever go to the Lebanon?' Anna asked, taking his hand off her breast. Philip shrugged his shoulders and attempted another ploy.

'He goes all over the place, to the Lebanon, to Hong Kong, even to Oxford and Cambridge and other minor foyers of learning.' His hand was now investigating another part of her anatomy but she took deft evading action.

'Does he still ... I mean, is he still an agent?'

'How should I know? I doubt it. Anyway, who cares? Everyone knows who he is and what happened. There's nothing secret about George Mado, so I can't see what use he could be. I mean a spy is supposed to be a sort of faceless operator, isn't he? Groping about in the dark?'

She took his hand away from its further exploration and tried to satisfy him with a conventional hug.

'Yes,' she said, 'I can see whose son you are but I don't like being groped about in the dark. In my country everyone has been groping about in the dark since I was born. In Czechoslovakia almost everyone is a spy for something or other. Everyone is a faceless operator. So who can you ever trust? But I'm now in England, Philip, where everyone trusts everyone else and there are no secret police.'

'You can't trust my father,' Philip said bitterly, 'and that's for sure.'

She gave him another long, passionate kiss and then broke firmly away.

'Well, I like him,' she said.

2

The British attitude to their public servants is a love-hate relationship, exasperating to foreigners and frequently inexplicable to the natives. We admire their probity and knock their behaviour in one breath, pay them reasonably well on active service and then make their pensions a hideous farce. George Mado, who in any case had never had a high regard for the Establishment, was now finding out just what it was like to be on the way out. This initially was no fault of his own. An accident had occurred and he had been arrested in Warsaw. The charge was trumped up, the trial secret and the sentence by Soviet standards unusually mild.

Mado, however, saw it in another light. Someone had shopped him. The event had taken place over three years ago at the time when Paul Tarnham, a high official of the Foreign Office, had defected, leaving behind him a wife and two children, a mystery as to why he had gone at all, since he had not apparently been spying for the Russians, and a wreckage of careers amongst his former colleagues, principally Rupert Eynsham the Head of his department at the Foreign Office at the time of his going.

One by-product of this, possibly coincidental, had been the quick shuffling around and in some cases the disappearance of various British agents operating on the continent of Europe. The Establishment referred to this as 'a routine reorganization'. Mado put it another way – 'The poor bastards have all been blown,' and from then on it had become a growing obsession of his to discover how this had happened and who was responsible.

'Because don't kid yourself he isn't still there, right at

the heart of things,' he said to Padstow, soon after arriving in Beirut.

'Who is?'

'Your actual super-Philby, the king boll weevil of them all. The epicentre will have changed that's all, the weak spot in the fabric where the next earthquake is going to break out.'

Padstow was the department's man in Beirut. He was young, eager to please and in Mado's view 'upper-class thick'. This was his first foreign appointment and he was damn well going to make a success of it. To Mado he was all that was wrong with the British in general and the outfit in particular.

Mado was looking at him with dislike across his double scotch in the seedy bar of the third-rate hotel in which his circumstances forced him to stay.

'I'll bet you thought the Visa Section actually issued visas,' Mado said.

'Well, we do, don't we? I mean – look – I don't really think we should be talking like this in a public place.'

'You imagine that what you do here isn't known to the Russians?'

'No, but nevertheless ...'

'So freak out, son. I can tie my own shoelaces now.'

'Well, I mean, I'm supposed to see you're all right. Er ... keep an eye on you, so to speak.'

'You do that,' Mado said, 'but do it from your desk. Tell them I'm up to my usual tricks. Drinking too much and laying anything in sight.'

'Yes,' Padstow said. It was regrettably true and this disconcerted him. He had no wish to show it. He knew he was supposed to keep control of the situation but Mado was notoriously hard to control. 'And do you think you'll actually sell any books to the American University?' he added lamely.

'It'll be a poor look-out if I don't,' Mado said, ordering another drink for himself. 'How else do you think I live?

I'm not working for your outfit now, you know, I'm not on the payroll.'

'Oh!'

'Didn't they tell you I've been pensioned off? A secret agent is supposed to be secret. There are one or two million people around who know who I am. So I'm not much use on that score, am I?'

'I suppose not. Well, I mean, you could have asked for a desk job, couldn't you?'

'That's right, sport, I could have asked for a desk job. And when you work out the answer to that one, we'll have another drink.'

Charmless clot, Padstow thought, as he walked back to the Embassy, no wonder he's in a mess. The nether side of the work, which covered Mado and his activities, had never seemed consonant in his mind with the Embassy life he enjoyed. He was far more at home chatting up his opposite numbers at cocktail parties at the Czech or Roumanian Embassies – real enemy territory if you wanted to put it in 007 terms – than trying to keep a character like George Mado on the straight and narrow.

'And in any case,' he complained to his secretary when making a note of this encounter, 'what did he mean by saying he wasn't working for us any more? What about Operation Powder Train? Isn't that why he's here in Beirut?'

Mrs Potts, the elderly secretary to the 'outfit', buried her head in the filing cabinet to hide her amusement. She liked Padstow and his Harrovian charm but doubted he had a great future in Intelligence.

'Wasn't Mado mentioned in the telegram we had about Powder Train, Mrs Potts?' Padstow repeated, wondering why he could never bring himself to call her Veronica instead of by her more formal nomenclature. 'Veronica' somehow implied an intimacy and that was a chilling thought with the lady in question. It would be like having it off with the matron at school.

'Yes, he was. But don't you think, if perhaps you were being observed, that a noisy disclaimer of that kind might be a necessary precaution? After all, George Mado is a very old hand at the game. He's hardly likely to talk about Powder Train in a bar in Ras Beirut.'

'Yes, Mrs Potts, I see what you mean.'

He paused unhappily until he did actually see what she meant. 'Now what's in the book for tomorrow?'

'You're lunching with that attaché you met at the Swiss Embassy the other day, Jean-Pierre Mournier, and in the evening there's Sheik Abdul ben Azzaman's reception at the Hilton.'

'Oh! Lord!' Padstow said, 'it's unending, isn't it? There ought to be danger money for the social chores we have to endure in Beirut. Am I never going to have a weekend off to myself?'

'Giorgio, you must get me back to the university by five,' Graziella said. 'Absolutely – definitely must – or I'll be in desperate trouble.'

Mado smiled as he drove the hired car north out of Beirut to one of the lonely beaches where at this time of year he knew they could be by themselves.

'There's no other way you could be in desperate trouble?' he answered.

'It's a little late to ask that sort of question, isn't it? No. You don't have to worry. I've been on the Pill since I was sixteen.'

'And what are you now? Sixteen and a half?'

'I was seventeen last month. Are you sure you can get me back? If my father knew I cut a lecture he'd be livid. My father is determined I should get my degree.'

'I'll get you back. Relax.'

'Thank you, Giorgio, I intend to.'

He took in her dark hair and olive skin, her good teeth and her young voluptuous thighs with approval. The Lebanese girls of today had left the yashmak a long way behind.

'I thought you had an Italian mother,' he said. 'Surely Catholics don't approve of the Pill for their young?'

'You must be joking,' she said, 'Mother was a Communist. Actually, Father's much stricter than she is.'

'Lebanese fathers usually are,' Mado said with a laugh, 'however politically sophisticated they may pretend to be.'

He hadn't felt so young for years. Only God – or Allah – knew how he was going to pay for the car, but for the moment he put his money troubles out of his mind. When they reached the bay he had chosen, they bathed though the March sea was still a little too cold for pleasure. Then they made love in the dunes.

'Where did you get that scar?' she asked when his thoughts were lulled with pleasure.

'I had a car crash a few years ago.' Some 'car crash', he thought, remembering with a sudden shiver the grey brutality of the Lubyanka prison. 'I damn nearly died,' he added.

'Well, don't crash us on the way home. They aren't the world's best drivers around here, you know.'

'I've noticed,' he said drily, admiring her composure. She was going to go far, this one. He wondered idly when the Phoenician element would come into play. A girl like Graziella had other things in mind than straight sex with a man of her father's age. It came sooner than he expected.

'Can you really get me a good agent and a screen test when I go to England?' she said, giving him a sharp look. 'I thought you were an educationalist.'

'I am. But I have powerful friends in the film business.'

'I bet that's what you say to them all.'

'No. As a matter of fact I've only just thought it up.'

She laughed and then said quickly:

'What are you up to in Beirut?'

'Selling books – and making love to you.'

'Is that all?'

Now it was his turn to laugh.

'Why? Have you got to turn in a report to your local committee?'

She sat up, startled and suddenly afraid. The Playboy view from the beach was magnificent.

'How did you know?'

'I didn't,' he said, kissing her breasts, 'I simply made an intelligent guess.'

She shivered and drew away.

'I think I'd like to go back.'

'Right,' he said, putting on his clothes. Then a wave of compassion struck him. 'Don't worry, love. You're a sweet girl and I wasn't just having you on. When you get to Oxford, I'll see you get a chance at the movies, if that's what you really want.'

It moved him that she cried to herself quite quietly on the way back. They were starting them young these days, he thought grimly, as they reached Beirut.

Dinkworthy and the Chief of his section, Sir Graham Corby, had a number of safe meeting places but, as they were both members of the same club in Pall Mall, had got into the habit of transacting their business over lunch and a drink. So far as other members of the club were concerned, their jobs had no connexion and they simply met casually whenever they both happened to be in the club together.

Dinkworthy was attached to the Ministry of Education and was known to have something to do with university grants. The Chief was believed to have been seconded from Shell to the Cabinet Offices as some sort of ill-defined adviser to the Government on the Middle and Far East. Nobody quite knew and nobody really cared. Since he was known to bumble about Downing Street, it was thought quite natural that he should have direct access to the Prime Minister but nobody gave a damn. It had always been bad form in that club to talk shop. Thus their conversation at the bar, the big table or wherever else they could be overheard usually concerned fishing and philately in which they both had an interest. Occasionally after lunch they would take coffee and a brandy together and it was then that they worked to an agenda known to both of them before such meetings ever took place.

Today they had simply to arrange where to see each other – and more important where not to meet – on a forthcoming trip to Hong Kong and Peking. They never travelled together and could always be genuinely astonished to come across each other accidentally in Teheran or other staging posts in different parts of the world. In fact, the real point of these separate journeys was the development of an operation known as Powder Train, the object of which was to foment and manipulate student unrest in the Communist satellites in the hope that once well and truly alight the fuse would lead straight into Soviet Russia itself.

Both Dinkworthy and his Chief knew exactly whom they were going to see and what each was trying to achieve. When it came to Beirut, Dinkworthy said:

'In view of the report on Mado, I think he ought to be dropped.'

'He has been.'

'Ah! ... moneywise too?'

'Money and every other wise. He's a dead loss. I was afraid this might happen. He's simply reverted to type. Liquor, baby dolls and straight self-indulgence. Stevens reports he was amply and appropriately warned. Now he's been cut off from the end of this month.'

'He's asked to go to Hong Kong,' Dinkworthy said.

'Well, if he does he's on his own and he hasn't the cash. He can stop where he is till the money runs out and then it's the same for him as for anyone else.'

'Do we get him home?'

'I don't think so,' the Chief said. 'He's of negative value – as God knows he has been for years.'

'What do you suppose he'll do?'

'Get some sort of local job, I suppose, and drink himself into the ground.'

'I agree it isn't for the want of warning,' Dinkworthy said. 'I've even had a word with him myself. He's a Queen's Hard Bargain, if ever there was one. Plus the fact that he's always so bloody rude.'

'I didn't appreciate you'd had direct contact with him,' the Chief said, giving Dinkworthy a sudden penetrating look. 'That wasn't the idea at all.'

'Oh! there hasn't been that sort of leak,' Dinkworthy said somewhat hurriedly. 'He connects me purely and simply with universities and education. He doesn't know I have anything at all to do with our section in general and Powder Train in particular – and of course your identity has been kept completely secure.'

'Ah!' the Chief said, looking into the distance, 'then how did you get your warning across?'

'We met accidentally at Oxford on that trip I took with the Czech Cultural Attaché, Patoček. Mado had been seeing his son who's up at Keble. After Patoček had gone to bed, I bumped into Mado and we had a nightcap together. Of course I made out that I only knew what the world knew about the Mado story, but I am a civil servant in the Ministry of Education. So I gave him a little Establishment talk. A sort of generalized friendly warning on the old-boy frequency.'

'How did he react?'

'As he always has done to others in the past. He has this obsession about being betrayed. He was abusive, of course. He informed me in barrack-room language that *he* wasn't a civil servant, never has been and never would be. He then told me what the Establishment could do with itself.'

The Chief smiled at the thought.

'And did he have any new ideas?'

'I didn't minute his proposals,' Dinkworthy said. 'I didn't think the Treasury would approve his suggestions, which were of a somewhat intimate and personal nature.'

'It's a pity all the same. If only he'd come to his senses in time. Still, he was quite generously treated after we got him back from Russia. We don't need to have him on our conscience now.'

3

Towards the end of March Mado began to sense that things were rapidly coming to a head in his life. By now he knew most of the signs. He had been given a modest travelling allowance by the consortium of educational publishers for whom he worked but they paid by results and these, in the Arab States and the Lebanon, had not been arrestingly good. The money was running out fast. Mado's reaction, as always, was to drink more heavily than ever and lay any girl he could get his hands on. This, in Beirut, as he had already discovered, was none too difficult. However, it did require a lubrication of money.

He had taken to getting up late and breakfasting off a prairie oyster. Graziella had not been able to repeat their afternoon on the beach. Her father, she said, had discovered she had missed a lecture. He had been furious and she thought she was now being watched. However, they were still able to see each other at the Student Club where they had originally met.

The Ras-el-Tin Culture Club was housed in a somewhat decrepit Turkish palace on the fringe of the old Arab quarter. It was run by a hook-nosed Lebanese promoter with the unlikely name of Ulf Achmed Azziz, the product some fifty years previously of an Arab father and a Swedish governess. The students for whom the club primarily existed called him the Avuncular Vulture, both because of his looks and because of his predatory habits so far as money and a profit to himself were concerned.

Mado had come across him by accident. A friendly bookseller whose order had scarcely been worth the shoe-leather getting it, suggested that Mado paid a visit to a record shop in Ras Beirut, in the back room of which he would find, if admitted, Mr Ulf Achmed Azziz.

'You won't sell any of the books you are travelling at present,' he said, 'at least not the ones you've shown me. Mr Azziz has other lines in which you might be interested and a large student clientele. He's really the Porn King of Beirut and he runs a Culture Club on the side.'

Mado and Azziz hit it off together as soon as they met, though neither revealed this fact to the other. Both knew they were birds of a feather, but this feeling was never put into words. Later that evening Azziz had taken him along to the Ras-el-Tin which was a mixture of Oxford Street discothèque, Soho blue-film club and 'Western respectable'. In the upper rooms of the palace Azziz had arranged some reasonably elegant public rooms, amongst which was a library, to give the whole operation the style and respectability its name required.

'Why Culture Club?' Mado had asked after inspecting the stock and the operation.

'Have you not noticed that present day Beirut is blessed with large numbers of military and diplomatic advisers from Eastern Europe and Russia? After the Six-Day War not everyone was on the Israeli side. Our Soviet friends are enormously interested in culture. Western sophisticates might say they have a long way to catch up in that line but certainly culture is not only a question of the Bolshoi Ballet and the Red Army Choir. Culture is enlightenment and Allah has made it possible for me to enlighten our Soviet friends in directions which are closed to them – or certainly in short supply – in their own country.'

'You charge all this up to Allah?'

'His ways are mysterious,' said Azziz, bowing in the direction of Mecca, 'and sometimes those who seek enlightenment are in need of a guide. This is occasionally my role. Were you to stay in Beirut perhaps you could assist me in this exacting and profitless task.'

'On a commission basis?'

'Ah!' said Ulf Achmed Azziz, giving him a sharp look from his hooded eyes, 'I see Allah has sent me someone with a highly developed business sense.'

'Right again, sport, and not one who would take his commission in kind or defer it.'

Mr Azziz sighed as if he had suffered disappointment. 'Money is certainly still the root of all evil,' he remarked, 'but in some lines it is often more lucrative to take one's commission in kind.'

'I have never pushed drugs,' Mado said tersely, 'and I never will.'

Mr Azziz shrugged his shoulders and looked into the distance.

'It is, of course, unthinkable that our Russian military friends should be interested in such Western decadencies as hashish, but there are students all over the world – even in Russia – who are hooked on these things, regrettable as it may seem to the authorities. I am not a philanthropist. I am not in the educational-book business, Mr Mado, I cater for other requirements. A train of events – particularly with the younger generation these days – can start in the unlikeliest circumstances and lead to the most unpredictable result. We both of us deal with students, Mr Mado, in our different ways and perhaps we may find our interests lie closer than at first sight appears. In any event I am happy to make you an honorary member of my club. The entrance fee for those over twenty-one is a mere twenty dollars, payable in cash, though in your case I would be happy to offset this sum against future commissions.'

'Great!' said Mado, 'now I know where I am.'

Ulf Achmed Azziz had not actually mentioned the words Powder Train but he had come perilously near to it.

The trouble was going to be getting out of his hotel. Already they were giving him the kind of look which told him they suspected the truth. He had cabled for a further advance but this had been simply ignored. He had his air ticket back to London and this he tried to trade in. But the airline merely said it would have to be credited back in London to the firm who had bought it for him. Soon he was down to his last ten pounds.

He went to see Padstow.

'I've got to go on to Hong Kong, can you fix up the travel-voucher side?'

Padstow made no attempt to hide his delight.

'It was you yourself who said you were no longer working for our outfit. You're not on the payroll.'

'I could very easily go back if I chose.'

'That's nothing to do with me.'

'You told me you were supposed to keep an eye on me. That must mean something even in Beirut.'

'You were kind enough to tell me to do so from my desk.'

'You're at your desk now. Come on, sport, see it my way. Put it on a 568D.'

This was the form used to requisition money on the secret fund.

'I'm sorry, Mr Mado, it can't be done.'

'I'll see the Ambassador myself,' Mado said as he swung out of the room, but this, he knew, could be nothing but an empty threat. He was on his own.

It began to look as if he would have to ask Azziz for a job. Even that was in doubt. The Vulture was not necessarily going to be avuncular so far as he was concerned. It might have been imagination but it now seemed to him as if those hooded eyes conveyed an idea of crafty triumph. Azziz was a sort of Shylock before the fall. He would want his pound of flesh.

Even Graziella with her feminine instinct for power had withdrawn into her cool seventeen-year-old Middle Eastern self. Desperate though he was, it still made him smile. When a crisis boiled up, it was power and not sex which women were after.

'But surely you have money in England?' she said

when she learnt that now he could not even buy her a drink.

'What makes you think that?'

'The British must have given you money when they got you back from Russia.'

'I have a divorced wife. I have a son to educate. The trust fund took it all.'

'You also drink a lot.'

He let this pass. She was also going to be a madam all right. If she didn't make it in the movies, she'd end up running a cosmetic business – or even a brothel. It stood out a mile.

'I don't think you should bother with England,' he said. 'Go straight to the States. You'll do better there.'

'Maybe I will. Why don't you ask your powerful friends in the film business for a job?'

'You're full of bright ideas tonight. I happen to be in Beirut. Not where the film business is.'

'Well,' Graziella said, tossing her head impatiently, 'if I were in your shoes, I wouldn't sit around a town like this drinking myself to pieces.'

'What would you do?'

'Work. Sell myself. Push a few pills, I wouldn't just sit and drink.'

He had many faults but self-pity was not amongst them. In the grey hangover mornings when the loneliness really bit deep, he could still draw strength from the fact that he had passed through far worse things in his life than running out of cash in Beirut. Something would happen. It always did. This bland and entirely private fatalism had been expensively bought. In the Lubyanka prison before he signed the confession they wanted, he had been reduced to sub-human level and had finally come to believe that he was going to be shot. The terror which had gripped him then fused his being in a new way. After facing that event nothing in the life to which he later returned could possibly be the same. He had had tempered into him not only a sort of personal survival kit but also an angry impatience, almost contempt of the ordinary life problems which hitherto had seemed insurmountable.

In the end nothing mattered except life itself. He was not a practising Christian but he now recognized the realities of some of the statements on which the faith relied. Faith was the evidence of things not seen. He did not know what he believed in but faith he had. And he had further come to know what it meant to give away your life in order to keep it. Something told him he was not going to stagnate in a Beirut bar for ever.

The next day and the one following no cable from London came about his money. On the third day a letter arrived saying that his sales figures were unsatisfactory and that he should return home forthwith. He had therefore to decide whether to obey this diktat or to ask Ulf Achmed for a job.

He began drinking in the late morning and by three was down to his last English pound. Just as he was about to go and seek out Azziz, he found that his glass had been refilled by a stranger who also picked up the chits by his elbow and settled them with the barman by handing them over with a sizable Lebanese note and a curt nod.

'I hope I may introduce myself by offering you a drink,' said the stranger. His English was correct but the accent was French. He extended his hand. 'I am Jean-Pierre Mournier and you are George Mado – yes?'

Mado was suddenly on his guard.

'You've got a nerve,' he said, bringing a hard concentration to bear on this dark, urbane young man. 'What can I do for you?' he went on, softening a little and playing for time. His long training came into play and a wary alertness beat the whisky fumes back into place.

'I'm sorry to break the ice so abruptly. But how does a stranger get to know you, Mr Mado?'

'How do you know my name?'

'That's not too difficult. Can we talk over there?'

Mado hesitated a moment.

'All right. What's it all about?' he said as they walked over to a quiet corner.

'I have a proposition to make you. I represent an important Foundation which is very interested in the work you are doing with young people, Mr Mado, especially students. We would like you to work with us. I think you will find the terms of the offer attractive.'

'What Foundation and what work?'

'The name doesn't matter. The work would be similar to what you are doing now.'

'I sell educational books.'

'Yes. You have quite an impressive list.'

'I'll be happy to take your order,' Mado said tersely. 'Let me have the Foundation's name and address.'

'You were going on to Hong Kong, I believe. Well, we would ask you to defer that part of your trip.'

'You seem to know the hell of a lot about me, Mr Mournier.'

No one was aware of the Hong Kong bit except London – and Padstow in the Embassy.

'What did you say you did?' Mado went on.

'I've told you my name. And we do indeed know a great deal about you, Mr Mado. You will have heard of Panayotis Marides, no doubt. I'm a friend of his. We work very closely together on certain matters of mutual interest. In point of fact he's here in Beirut at this moment. We hope you'll come to a little party he's giving tonight.'

Mado stared at him coldly and said nothing. Since none of his questions were answered, he decided to leave the running to this very self-possessed young man – with the powerful hands. There was a pause. The flies rotated endlessly over the greasy bar. An aged prostitute sized them up but got no response to her inviting look. Out in the street the sun beat down.

'Then in a few days Mr Marides goes back to Athens. Mrs Tarnham and her two children are coming out to spend a few days in Greece at his house. Mr Marides is a very generous man.'

At the mention of Tarnham's name Mado froze into complete stillness, a reaction the other noticed with a smile.

'Of course we all remember Paul Tarnham, don't we? Especially people like you who were thrown away at the time he defected. It was all a little unfortunate, wasn't it?'

'Unfortunate is the word.'

'And as I expect you know, Rupert Eynsham – who was his immediate Chief at the time and who didn't go with him – is now the Counsellor at your Embassy in Athens.'

'What is all this leading up to?'

'I've told you. We want you to work with us.'

'Where?'

'In Prague.'

'You must be out of your mind.'

'I don't think so,' Mournier said blandly. 'I was with Paul Tarnham a few days ago in Prague. He's very anxious to meet you.'

In spite of the training Mado showed a flicker of surprise.

'So that's where he fetched up, did he?'

'Yes. You will find Prague a fascinating place to work in these days. Spring 1968 will go down as the beginning of a vintage year.'

'You must be out of your mind,' Mado repeated, 'if you seriously think I would work for the KGB.'

'You would not be working for the KGB,' Mournier interrupted, 'you would be usefully assisting the Czechs to liberalize their régime. That's a very different matter indeed.'

'Listen, sport. I was blown when Tarnham defected, as you've just pointed out. I was nicely worked over in Russia, beaten up, tortured and damn nearly shot. If you think I'd ever expose myself to that sort of thing again, you need your head examined.'

'But I am right in assuming, am I not, that you still nurture an intense desire to find out who gave you away, to discover the identity of the man in your organization whom you describe as the "super Philby" – who is still there today?'

Mado nodded reluctantly. He was forced to admire Mournier's nerve.

'We can help you along those lines.'

'You know yourself?'

'I said we could help you to find out yourself.'

'Prove it.'

Mournier shook his head and smiled like a cat.

'Really, Mr Mado, a man of your experience should know better than to ask naïve questions of that kind.'

This stung him into anger.

'You could perfectly well be making this up. Most of the facts you've given me are public knowledge. Add a little intelligent guesswork and you're in business as a stool pigeon. Come off it, Mr Mournier, I'm not as naïve as all that.'

'Operation Powder Train isn't public knowledge, though, is it?' he said quietly. Then he lit a cigarette and blew out the smoke. There was a long pause. Out in the street an Arab vendor gave one of his strange selling cries. In the distance a dog incessantly barked.

'Is that perhaps the proof you required?' Mournier eventually said. This time it was Mado's turn to avoid answering directly.

'I don't know if you've ever been in a Russian prison, my friend, but take it from me you get a five-star treatment there with experts in every department. Once in a lifetime is enough for any man, if he's lucky to get out alive.'

'Listen, Mr Mado, there isn't much time. I am a very busy man and we know that you are, too – when it suits you to be. You also have courage. Now I must speak plainly. I haven't come to this salubrious bar just for fun. You are no longer paid a salary by the British Security

Service – though you might reasonably expect some ex-gratia payment if the Powder Train is ignited. All this we know. In the meantime the gratuity they gave you when you got back from Russia has long since gone – and I know all about your wife at Camberley and your son at Oxford. You are discredited and disreputable, out of work, drunk, lecherous and quite possibly diseased. You have failed to sell enough books to pay for this trip, you have no means of getting on to Hong Kong and no money there, if you were to arrive. You can't even leave this elegant hotel. Wouldn't it be wise at least to consider my offer? You can let me know the answer at the party tonight.'

'Thanks for the biography,' Mado said. 'Run through that catalogue again and cheer me up.'

But Mournier continued to press.

'What would induce you to work for us on the lines suggested?'

'I'll tell you,' Mado said grittily. 'A *laissez-passer* signed by Brother Brezhnev and twenty thousand pounds in a nice clean Swiss bank in a nice clean numbered account.'

Mournier gave a short laugh.

'I told you before and I'll tell you again. You would not be working for the Russians. You must also be aware that twenty thousands pounds is very much above what you would be worth in any market in the world. I can get you a passport signed by Comrade Dubček, if you like, and possibly five thousand pounds. Czechoslovakia is desperately short of foreign currency.'

'And desperately short of double agents,' Mado added.

'There would be nothing double about your agency,' Mournier said in a steely tone of voice, 'be absolutely sure about that. See you at the Marides party around eight o'clock. I think you know the address.'

Then with an agility which impressed, Mournier slipped quickly away into the hot afternoon sunlight of Beirut.

4

The immediate effect on Mado was to sober him up and make his brain race. Soon after Mournier had gone, he left the bar himself and began walking along the front, past the St George Hotel where in more moneyed times he would have been staying. He needed to digest what had just taken place.

Beirut with its palm trees and expensive shops had never been a place in which to be penniless and at risk. Normally he would have rented a car and driven up into the mountains to clear his head and work it all out. Now that he was broke, he had no alternative but to walk, and by six o'clock he had traversed and retraversed the whole of the town.

He was in a bad way. That this was nobody's fault but his own gave him scant consolation and even less help. In one damning sentence Mournier, whoever he was and whatever he really intended, had summed up his present condition. He was rotten, discredited and clobbered. If he were not to accept Mournier's dangerous and questionable offer, he had no alternative but to go to Azziz. Or he could force the Embassy to get him back to England. Like it or not – and Padstow quite clearly wasn't going to help – they would have to advance him enough money to pay his hotel bill and get him away. But this was no general solution.

He sat down on a bench and stared at the sea. Who was this Mournier? And what was behind it all? They undoubtedly had the facts. Mournier had been superlatively briefed. To find out about Mado's life and present condition was not difficult. But to reveal the code name of the current operation which was in progress gave Mado one more sickening proof that the service must have been penetrated right at the top. If Philby had gone down to history as the third man, if Tarnham had perhaps been the fourth – then the fifth and sixth and so on were still undiscovered and quite obviously still at work.

This dire fact worked on him, as it always did, to bring the fight back into him and to banish despair. He did not trust Mournier and the danger of again going behind the Iron Curtain was incalculable, present and arrestingly real. However, he had lived with risk for as long as he could remember. It could still pay off, if the money-to-risk ratio happened to be attractive.

Abruptly he stood up and made his way to Azziz's record shop. There would be no harm in hedging the bet. The Vulture greeted him with a smile.

'I was wondering when you would come,' he said.

'I'm broke and I want a job.'

'I know. Things get around in Beirut. However, I am not an employment agency, Mr Mado.'

'Not even for a good-looking temp like me?'

'What are you suggesting you could do for me that I should pay you money?'

'I could run the Ras-el-Tin for you.'

'Thank you, I run it perfectly well myself.'

'You yourself suggested a little time back that I might work with you on a commission basis.'

'Yes, but you made an immediate condition which rather blunted my interest.'

'Ah!' said Mado, 'that was the idea for yesterday. To-day is another day.'

'I'll think about it,' Azziz said, standing up and edging Mado to the door.

'I'm seeing Panayotis Marides tonight, perhaps that might be of interest to you as well.'

'Oh! it is, indeed it is. But then I knew that already.' He paused for a moment to let the effect of this sink in. 'Mr Marides is a hard man to do business with. Very rich men so often are. But it was nice of you to look in, Mr Mado. Do keep in touch.'

Panayotis Marides was a Greek millionaire who had made his money out of shipping but who now had diverse interests all over the world. He was not without charm but he had kept the peasant shrewdness with which he had been born and his pleasure these days lay mainly in the exercise of power.

Although he had houses all over the world, he did not bother with one in Beirut but instead borrowed the palace of an oil-fired sheik with whom he did business. This was an imposing white building in the Beirut millionaires' row, with a magnificent garden, and Mado smiled ironically at the contrast this ambiance made with the seedy hotel which had been his own background for the last few weeks.

The drive was full of cars when he arrived. Evidently the party had been going on for some time and it struck Mado that perhaps he had been invited late on purpose. He wondered why. Maybe they thought he might fall down drunk on the floor if he had been asked along at the start of the party. Mournier, who was with a group of young people, spotted him and came across. At first sight everyone at the party appeared to be young.

'I'm so glad you could make it,' he said, offering his hand. 'Now relax – you are among friends.'

'I seem to be late.'

'No one is late. This party's been going on for twenty-four hours and can well go on for another two days. People just come and go. Marides likes it that way. It's his style. *Boeuf bourguignon* is one of his favourite dishes. He loves the different sauces you dip your meat in. Come on over and I'll introduce you.'

'Hallo, Giorgio, fancy seeing you here,' Graziella said as he passed a marble pillar. She and a coloured boy of her own age were leaning up against the pillar. Instinctively he knew they were high.

'Yes, fancy,' he said, winking at her and continuing across the room.

Panayotis Marides turned out to be a swarthy, somewhat stocky little man who looked every inch the dynamic tycoon the world knew him to be. He was clearly enjoying himself. Success had enabled him to indulge his taste for women and there were plenty of pretty girls around that night. Marides had divorced his wife some time ago in a manner satisfactory to both. His wife lived in Paris but they saw each other from time to time whenever Marides considered that their differing worlds should be brought together.

This was not one of the occasions. He had a son in the Greek Foreign Office, a dark, good-looking, vicious young man, who was with him now. Mado observed that once he had been identified to Marides, Mournier disappeared watchfully into the background. Not only agile, Mado concluded, but a chameleon into the bargain. Mournier and the Marides son looked as if they were wary and dangerous men. If all three were working together, it was clearly a combination not to be underestimated.

'I am delighted you could come,' Marides said in faultless English and then dropped into the Greek-American accent he sometimes affected to embarrass strangers. 'Itsa the malt whisky you like, Mr Mado, issa correct? Endax, we fixa you one proper drink.'

A servant in a white gallabieh instantly whisked away Mado's glass and replaced it with an unblended whisky such as Mado had not tasted in years. Marides watched him and saw his approval.

'Itsa good way you take him neat,' he said and then again in ordinary English, 'Never adulterate a spirit of that quality with water – but then I'm talking to an expert.'

He turned to the sombre-looking Chinese on his right.

'If you were ever to need an adviser on scotch in Peking,' he said, 'I am sure you would find Mr Mado of value. Mr Mado is going to help me with my Educational

Foundation,' he went on to a tall, grey-haired man in thick, horn-rimmed spectacles. 'Allow me to present you, George, if I may call you that, to the Head of the Special Trade Mission to the Lebanon, Mr Novaček. I think you met his daughter when you were recently in Oxford – isn't that so?'

Mado nodded with a smile and politely shook hands. He wondered what else about him was known. I also buy my shirts at Marks and Spencers, he said to himself, they should make a note of that. These were no amateurs. They had not only checked him up in depth, they knew how best to use their knowledge. The timing was exact and effective. He had scarcely arrived yet in a sense they already had him at bay.

There was a short pause. Then the Czech, who also spoke excellent English, turned to him and said casually:

'My daughter's coming along later tonight. She's using the Easter vacation to get in a little skiing in the Lebanon. As a matter of fact I invited your son to come out with her as well, but he couldn't make it. Apparently he's a member of a pop group and they use the vacation to tour. Such a pity they couldn't come. But perhaps we can invite them to Prague.' He paused and smiled. 'Prague is an interesting place, Mr Mado, especially today.'

'And he means this very day,' Marides put in quickly. 'Yesterday Mr Novotny finally disappeared from the scene. Comrade Dubček and his friends are riding high.' He shot a quick glance at Mr Novaček. 'Who knows who will be the Tito of Czechoslovakia?'

The Czech did not appear to have heard. In any case Mado found it impossible to gauge what he thought. Mr Novaček had the professional diplomat's ability at parties to seem not to have taken in remarks which might require an embarrassing reaction. Mado became aware that Marides' attention was on himself and that he had perhaps intended the last remark to provoke an answer from him. So be it, he thought, and gave Marides the lead he wanted.

'There won't be a Tito of Czechoslovakia,' Mado said, watching both their faces. 'The Russians would never allow it.'

'How do you suppose they would prevent it?' Marides asked silkily with a glance at the silent Chinese on his right.

'The Russians can do what they like – in any of the countries they control.'

'You think they'd use force as they did in Hungary twelve years ago?'

'They will never allow another Tito,' Mado said firmly.

'Well ...' Marides concluded with a cruel smile, 'you certainly know the Russians better than some of us here. But I think you should meet other associates of mine in the Educational Foundation.'

He turned and said something inaudible to Mournier. Then with a brief smile at Mado, he slipped his hand under Novaček's elbow and guided him away to another part of the room.

'An impressive man,' Mournier remarked when he and Mado were again alone. 'Like all great men – all great entrepreneurs, he never permits political frontiers or ideologies to stand in the way of business.'

'Come on outside,' Mado said, leading the way to the terrace where they could talk without being overheard. 'You and friend Marides seem to assume I've accepted your offer ... I haven't.'

'What offer, Giorgio?' Mournier said blandly. Both of them could see Graziella, who had not moved from the pillar except to sit down with her dreamy friend. Mournier's use of the word 'Giorgio' neatly lasered the connexion between him and the girl.

'What offer indeed? I would not consider going to Prague unless and until I get a passport by Dubček and five thousand pounds in cash here in my hand. I'll see to the Swiss banking end myself.'

'And then you would help us with Powder Train?'

'I'll tell you then.'

'The passport will take two days, but I have already put it in hand. The money you can have tonight – although it would be easier all round if you can restrain your impatience until business hours tomorrow.'

'Tomorrow is Sunday.'

'But we are in Beirut.'

'So fix the money tonight.'

Mournier gave him a hard look.

'You are certainly a gambler, Giorgio. If that's the way you want it ...'

'Anyone can be a gambler, Mr Mournier, when his life is at stake.'

With another cheerless smile Mournier seemed to melt away, leaving him with his hands on the balustrade staring out at the garden in the foreground with the lights of Beirut beyond. He felt intensely alone. There were so many different ways of dying. Other moments in his life when danger and despair had dominated his being came drifting back into his thoughts. He remembered his arrest in Warsaw after the Tarnham defection, and the realization earlier on that in the trade he had adopted no one could be trusted.

You were always alone. It had been this factor more than anything else which had wrecked his marriage and destroyed his personal life. 'You're not a particularly evil man,' his wife had said when they had decided to divorce, 'I simply don't know where I am with you, that's all. And now I don't care. Set up the trust fund you've always talked about and get out of my life.'

In the world of espionage, friendship and trust were the rarest, most valuable things in your life. In one sense it was all you had left. Until his arrest he had still trusted one or two people with whom he had worked, still felt he had one or two friends on whose integrity he could always rely. Tarnham had put an end to that.

As his glass was empty he decided to get it refilled. There now seemed to be more people than ever milling about the marble-floored room with its grand piano at one end and the Impressionist paintings on the walls. More than half of them appeared to be students of Graziella's age. His private respect for Marides grew. There was a blending of talent at this party which would have done honour to a medieval Florentine court.

He found the servant who knew about the unblended scotch and relaxed a little. He was just reaching into his pocket for his cigarettes when a girl's voice said:

'Have one of mine, Mr Mado.'

He turned to find Annabella Novaček smiling at him. She had had her blonde hair cut fashionably short and the mini-skirt had now moved up to pelmet level. She looked disarmingly fresh.

'You don't remember me,' she went on, 'but we met for a moment in an Oxford bar.'

'Of course I remember you,' Mado said. 'My son warned me off the course. In any event your father said you would be here tonight.'

He did not tell her in words how pleased he was to see her, but his eyes conveyed the message. She responded with a smile which seemed to envelop him, and gave him great pleasure.

'Philip was very angry that night. He said you'd be making a pass at me.'

'Yes,' Mado said, lighting their cigarettes, 'Philip long ago lost any respect for his father that he ever had. And that was his father's fault, I'm sorry to say.'

It was obvious she understood. The old tingling sexual chemistry was at work and both of them knew it.

'Philip's a friend but not my boyfriend,' Anna said, taking it on with a smile, 'so I don't hold it against you.'

'You should,' Mado countered, 'my son's quite right to feel as he does.'

'No,' she went on gravely like a child. 'I told him he was wrong to try and poison me against you. We are all of us free now to make up our own minds about people.

That's what's so good about 1968. That's one thing I learnt at Oxford.'

'I'm glad you enjoyed it. When are you going back?'

'I'm not. I'm doing a course at the Sorbonne. Then back in the autumn to Prague.'

Mado was aware of someone approaching him from behind.

'My dear fellow, what a surprise! Where will we meet next? Do introduce me to your friend.'

There was no mistaking that thinly smooth, dated voice. It struck him in passing that he and Annabella were fated to be interrupted. She gave him a quick understanding glint as they broke off the conversation.

'This is Simon Dinkworthy,' he said. 'Annabella Novaček.'

'Really! I've just been talking to your father. I didn't realize he had such a glamorous daughter.'

'Take care of this one,' Mado said wryly, 'in a moment or two he'll be making a pass at you. Like someone else you know. Never trust a man from the Ministry of Education, even if you do meet him in Beirut.'

The idea of Dinkworthy making a pass at anyone made him laugh out loud. Then, not wishing Dinkworthy to take over the lead in the conversation, he went on: 'Everyone seems to be here tonight. Who's that talking to Marides?'

'You don't mean Miss Patoček's father?'

'Novaček,' Anna said giving him a sharp startled look, which to Mado was like touching a live wire. He wondered why she was so surprised.

'I beg your pardon, I was confusing the name with your Cultural Attaché in London. You remember, my dear chap,' Dinkworthy went on easily to Mado, 'I introduced you when we last met at Oxford.'

'Yes,' Mado said firmly, 'I do remember and no, I don't mean Mr Novaček now. Who's the other one?'

'That's Sir Graham Corby,' Dinkworthy said, standing on his toes to get a better look. 'I believe I saw in the papers that he's been on some sort of fact-finding mission to Hong Kong. He's one of the PM's troubleshooters, you know. At least that's what we think he is.'

'We?'

'We both belong to the same club,' Dinkworthy said. 'and old Corbers has always been something of a mystery man. Used to be with Shell, I believe. Maybe he still is. He'll have met Marides that way.'

Mado wondered how best to get rid of Dinkworthy. Instinct drew him to Anna and he urgently wanted to talk to her alone. Maybe he could bore him off the course. He knew Dinkworthy found work a great tedium, so he asked him what he was doing in Beirut.

'Selection boards. Incessantly boring university selection boards,' Dinkworthy said and switched the inquiry to Mado.

'And have you had a successful trip? Let me see, you look after the Dobbs, Crowborough and White educational list, don't you?'

'Oh! yes,' Mado said, blithely lying. 'It's been highly successful up to date. You could say I've saturated the Lebanon with our textbooks. A firm sale of six copies – and I'm shortly going on to Hong Kong where I might sell another. Maybe I ought to have a word with Sir Graham Corby, if that's where he's been.'

He observed that Marides' son and Mournier had straddled Corby and had separated him from Marides. He wondered what significance lay in this part of the ritual dance.

'I'd be delighted to introduce you, old boy, but I don't think it would do you much good. Educational publishing and old Corbers are poles apart. He wouldn't have a clue what you were talking about. Now if you were to chat him up about stamps or fishing, you might get somewhere. But my impression of Corbers is that he's not exactly an intellectual. He more or less graduated from *Tiger Tim* to *Country Life* in one go for his reading matter and that was a long time ago.'

'You say he's some sort of troubleshooter for the PM?'

'What better, old boy? If you had anyone who could actually read in that outfit, the whole country would collapse.'

Mado observed that Marides was now walking the gloomy Chinese over to Corby. He also took note of the fact that the British Ambassador and Padstow had just arrived. Panayotis could certainly pull them in. And Tarnham's wife is going to stay with the Marides in Athens, Mado reflected, just for a holiday, just for a few simple days in Greece.

'Let me get you something to eat, Miss Novaček,' Dinkworthy was saying and had deftly piloted her away towards the room where the food was. She turned and gave Mado a quick, appealing look but there was nothing he could then do, so he smiled back and shrugged his shoulders.

'Ah! Mr Mado,' said Padstow with that inane smile which Nanny must once have told him was charming, 'a word in your ear. I have some heartening news.'

He and Dinkworthy would make a good pair, Mado thought, as they walked along the terrace together, a pair as up to the minute as the Western Brothers.

'I was going to ask you to look in at the Embassy on Monday,' Padstow said. 'I didn't think I'd bump into you tonight.'

'No. I appreciate this sort of party is more your preserve than mine. However, here I am. So hearten me up.'

'It may be possible to get you on to Hong Kong.'

If Padstow expected a reaction to this astonishing piece of news, he was disappointed. Mado never flickered for a second.

'What do you mean – "may be"? London has either given you authority or it hasn't.'

'Yes,' Padstow said reluctantly, 'to my great surprise.'

'You're in for some other surprises, sport, before you're through with this one. I need some drinking money as well.'

He thought Padstow might break down and cry. It must be very humiliating to have to backtrack over a nasty, dirty little bastard such as himself.

'Yes,' Padstow said again sadly. 'Well that's it, then, isn't it? Perhaps you'd be in my office at 10.30 on Monday.'

'Oh! no,' Mado said, 'you get it to me. At the hotel tomorrow.'

'But tomorrow's Sunday.'

'That's right. London would want it that way. And if you find me in bed with Graziella or her splendid boyfriend, don't make a sound. Just leave it on the mantelpiece and get the hell out of it.'

'Well, really ...' Padstow began but Mado had left him, and to his further dismay had gone over to Graziella, pulled her and her boyfriend to their feet and removed them towards the room where the dancing was taking place.

5

Bloody, arrogant, drunken idiot! Dinkworthy said to himself as he got away from Mado and steered this dumb Czech through what he called the milling throng. Why had London taken up with him again? Why couldn't they have let the fellow go, as the Chief had decreed before they set off on this trip? It would all be money down the drain and God knows what embarrassment he could cause them in Hong Kong, if he ever got there.

Who in London had countermanded the Chief's orders when his back was turned? He had only just heard about it from Padstow, a bright, well-spoken boy if ever there was one, before coming on to this vulgar, impossible party. There would be hell to pay when the Chief got back. It was all Dinkworthy could do not to go over to him now and ask what it was all about.

But in Beirut as in Singapore, he and Sir Graham Corby were on the coolest of casual terms. Indeed, except that they were both English and had probably been to the same public school, what connexion could there possibly be? There was some slight consolation, he supposed, in the fact that Mado appeared not to be aware of the real identity of either of them, otherwise he certainly would not have asked for an introduction to Sir Graham for a casual chat on Hong Kong.

'So you are educational?' Anna asked as they helped themselves to food. The better she knew English, the more mistakes she made on purpose to get a laugh. She did not imagine Dinkworthy was going to make her laugh.

'When it comes to pretty girls like you, I'm

educational,' Dinkworthy said with an appalling attempt at gallantry. In point of fact, although he had married and dutifully produced a family, he had always preferred the boys and had had one or two memorably larky experiences before legality took away all the fun from being secretly on the lavender side.

'And so is that man we were with just now? Educational, I mean?'

'I think it would be fair to say George Mado is – or certainly has been educational. He flogs books to unsuspecting book-buyers in schools and universities. But you know his son, don't you, at Oxford?'

Anna gave him another penetrating look and discovered to her surprise that Dinkworthy was expecting it and returned her an equally curious stare.

'Yes, I do. But how did you know that?'

'Your Cultural Attaché Novaček told me when I took him to Oxford.'

'Patoček. Novaček is my name.'

'Oh! yes,' Dinkworthy said with a giggle which his cold, calculating eyes completely denied. 'I'm so sorry. I'm always getting it wrong. I've got a brain like a sieve.'

Anna had always been an impulsive girl and Dinkworthy was the sort of hypocritical Englishman she most disliked. Afterwards she was to wonder why she reacted in this way, but for the moment a sort of anger made her take the bull by the horns.

'I don't think so, Mr Dogsbody. I think you have a very clear brain indeed and you strike me as a completely ruthless man – educational or otherwise.'

'I beg your pardon?'

His startled reaction gave her momentary pleasure.

'I don't think you accidentally confused our two names at all. You were simply covering up. You are quite as aware as I am who Mr Patoček is and what he does and always has done for a living. He is simply a spy. An informer. The sort of person I hope we shall soon see very much less of in Czechoslovakia.'

Dinkworthy had quickly recovered his bland imperturbability.

'Good Lord love us,' he said lightly, his tone of voice again being negated by his sub-zero eyes. 'Does your father know you're going around Beirut talking like this?'

'I'm not going round Beirut, as you put it. I'm saying it to you now because I think you're having me on, Mr Dagworth, and I don't like being made a fool of.'

'You've learnt to speak English very well in the few months you were at Oxford.'

'Yes,' said Anna crisply. 'We Czechs are like you were in 1940. We have to take care of ourselves. No one else is going to and there may not be a lot of time. Excuse me, now, I see my father would like to talk to me. Thank you for looking after me so well.'

Her father told her it was time to be going. Even a few months ago she would have obeyed without question. Now she produced the sort of look she had seen her mother give when defending 'her' theatre people in Prague against some pompous official requirement. She asked if she might stay a little longer. Her father raised his eyebrows and frowned.

'Why?'

'Just independence, Father, I'm enjoying myself.'

'All right, I'll send the car back for you. Don't let all this liberalism go to your head too much.'

She smiled, again managing to look much as her mother had done when she was an up-and-coming actress of Anna's age.

'Whose side are you on, Father? Us or them?'

The frown deepened.

'You must not talk like this even in our own language – not here.'

'Oh! I don't suppose this room is bugged and if it is whoever's listening must have a hard job picking things out. I won't stay long.'

Then to clinch it, she kissed him quickly – another

ebullient Western habit – and then equally quickly slipped away.

Jean-Pierre Mournier found it easy to detach Mado from Graziella and her Nigerian medical student. Mado was obviously the odd man out.

'One of the problems of the student revolution is going to be their reliability,' he said to Mado as they moved away. 'The powder mustn't be allowed to get damp, as it has tonight.'

He gave Mado a thickish envelope in an unobtrusive way.

'We thought you'd prefer it in thousand-franc notes. It's less bulky that way.' Then as an afterthought, 'Swiss francs, of course, in case you thought I was joking.'

Now that he had the money in his hand, a grinding sense of doom took possession of him, a sudden realization that this was the end of the road. He knew that Mournier was observing his hesitation and this added to the danger.

'I've changed my mind,' he said, giving the packet back. 'I told you earlier on I wouldn't decide until you got me the signed *laissez-passer*. Keep the money until then.'

'Just as you wish,' Mournier said silkily. 'This merely proves that we keep our side of the bargain. You asked for the money tonight. *Le voilà.*'

'Money's not everything,' Mado heard himself saying lamely. He knew he was making things worse but he did not seem able to help himself. It was like stumbling along a mountain path with a big drop on one side.

'It is in Beirut,' Mournier was as cool as ever. 'But don't think anything of it. Leave it a couple of days if you want. We thought you might find some ready cash useful now.'

'Thanks for the thought,' Mado said wryly. 'It's the thought that counts.'

'However, once the passport arrives,' Mournier continued, 'there can be no further delay.' The threat was plainly visible. 'You do understand, don't you?'

'You want me to say I get the message.'

'Yes.'

'Well, I do.'

'Enjoy yourself at the party.' Mournier began to glide away in his catlike manner. 'Mr Marides likes his guests to take away nice memories of the parties he gives.'

And why not? he said to himself. He fixed himself up with another respectable scotch and walked out into the garden. The cool night air was therapeutic. But therapeutic of what? And what was the real seat of the disease?

He thought back on his life as he had done so often before and tried to establish for his own satisfaction what it was all about. What had brought him to this point? Why, in fact, did he go on at all? Beirut was a great place to disappear from – either from a particular form of life or from life itself. What was holding him back?

'I thought I might find you out here,' Anna said, and slipped her arm into his as if they had been very old friends, perhaps even lovers. 'We never seem to get started, do we? I mean at getting to know each other. Someone always interrupts.'

'You should think twice about getting started with someone like me.'

'I have,' she said firmly. 'Don't worry, I can look after myself.'

'Yes,' he replied and kissed her wide, welcoming mouth. 'I think you can. However, that's not what it's about. At least not just at present it isn't.'

'No,' she agreed, drawing him closer. 'You need a friend.'

'Who doesn't?' he said, thinking of the number of women who had made a similar approach to him on his Iron Curtain trips. None had been as open and fresh as this one but all had been doing it under orders from the KGB. A quick memory of Graziella's expression on the beach flashed into his mind. They were certainly going for the young these days. First Graziella and now this warm, ample Slav with her youth and vitality. The bait was irresistible but he still played it cool. He was well past the time when sexual magnetism, however potent, could swing him off course. His present trouble, though, was to plot out for himself the particular course he was trying to follow. As if reading his mind, she said:

'You think I've been sent out here, don't you? To ensnare you in a very obvious way, if I can.'

'It did cross my mind.'

'Well, I haven't,' she said simply. 'I came to you of my own accord. And I don't care if you believe me or not. I think you need help.'

'And is that what your father feels?'

'I haven't discussed you with my father.'

'Patoček then?'

She drew slightly away.

'You're determined to give me the wrong motives, aren't you? You won't accept a gesture for what it's worth.'

He put his hands on her shoulders and looked her in the face.

'Wouldn't you – if you were me?'

She looked suddenly sad and deflated.

'I suppose so.'

'And it isn't quite as innocent as you'd have me believe, is it? When you were at Oxford, you were reporting to Patoček, weren't you?'

'But of course. It was a condition of the visa. However, what I reported was again something else. You know how it is in my country and in Russia.'

'Yes, I know how it is.'

There was a pause. The lights of Beirut twinkled in the background and from the house came the noise of the party which showed no sign of abating. She had such a fresh, powerful attraction for him he wanted to take her there and then. She gave him a little, appealing smile. Whatever the motive, she reciprocated the wild urgent pull he felt. But this was not yet the time. He deliberately extended the pause to draw her out.

'So you're not going to trust me after all,' she said eventually, like a disappointed child.

'It would help if you trusted me a little more. How much do you know?'

'Not much in detail. I do know you're going to be asked to help us with the student Powder Train.'

'Good God Almighty!' Mado exploded. 'They should advertise it in the Press.'

There was another pause.

'I'm in it too,' she said.

'So I gathered. And your father?'

'I doubt it very much. He's a Novotny man. A conservative. But mother is. She's already back in Prague. She's an actress.'

She was certainly telling the truth about the facts he knew.

'Then it strikes me you may need a friend as well.'

'We all do – if we're going to pull it off.'

Mado laughed.

'You students think you can do anything, don't you? Even topple the Kremlin.'

'Who else is going to do it? And it *can* be done. It's going to be done.'

He found her drive and enthusiasm touching and infectious. A million years separated them and yet they were astonishingly close.

'Don't lose your head,' he said. 'You'd better not be out here with me too long. Come on, I'll walk you back.'

'Can you remember a number? If you do come to Prague and want to reach me in a hurry, call 258612. Don't write it down.'

'258612.'

'And one other thing,' she said, 'but this is just an idea from the top of my head. I don't think you should trust the man who interrupted us before.'

'Simon Dinkworthy.'

'Yes. I don't think that could ever be a friend.'

'I wouldn't know about friendship. He's certainly a king-size twit.'

'What's a twit?'

'I've no idea how good your English really is but you could say it's the masculine of Twatt – and that's a town in the Orkneys.'

He had her there and that made him smile.

'I think the English are all basically mad,' Anna said, 'and that's why I love you all. Now don't forget – 258612. I mustn't keep the car, so now I must go.'

'Do I see you again?'

'Yes, please.' She gave him her dazzling smile.

'Like tomorrow we could go to the mountains or I could show you Baalbek.'

'Call me at the Embassy,' she said and went to the waiting car.

He had a few more drinks and then decided to go back to his dingy hotel. Graziella had already left with her coloured friend and Mado felt he had now had his fill of scotch for the night. Just as he was about to leave, Padstow came bustling up.

'A word in your ear, old chap,' he said, in what he fancied to be a casual manner.

'You had one earlier on, remember? I don't think I could stand an orgy.'

Padstow ignored the sarcasm, looked round in a hopelessly self-conscious way to see if they were being overheard or observed and then said confidentially:

'I wasn't going to say this to you except in the Embassy but part of the rethinking about your case seems to hinge on—'

'My case? What case? What are you talking about?'

'I mean London's decision to – er – assist you on to Hong Kong – well, one factor apparently is that you may possibly be approached by the – the other side.'

'You're telling me I should watch out in public lavatories for the next few days?'

'Nonsense,' Padstow said angrily. 'You know quite well what I'm getting at. Don't you?'

'Backs to the wall, boys, here comes Brezhnev. Is that it?'

'You're impossible. I knew you'd send up the whole idea. Well, I simply have to tell you that if you do get such an approach – it's not likely but just possibly on the cards – if you are at the receiving end of such an approach, London want to know absolutely instanter. Do I make myself clear?'

'You've done a good job, sport, and I mean that sincerely. Do I tell you first or go to Matron?'

'Well, really . . .' Padstow said and then turned abruptly away. There were times when he felt like chucking in the job. No wonder the stupid so-and-so got caught in Russia, he thought, as Mado strode off into the night a little unsteady in the gait.

6

In the event Mado was never able to tell Padstow or anyone else. They came for him in the middle of the night, about an hour or so after he had dropped off into a deep sleep. There were four of them in all, including the driver of the car. The first Mado knew of it was when he woke up looking straight into the barrel of a revolver.

'Get up, Mr Mado. Get dressed and packed.'

'Who are you?'

Even fighting his way back to consciousness through an alcoholic miasma, he knew quite well who they were. There was even a Russian smell in the room. They looked caricature thugs with their ridiculous greatcoats, except that as Mado felt the old, old fear gripping his stomach, he knew them to be only too real.

'No questions, and no noise. Otherwise ...'

He sat up and pushed the revolver aside. This was all horribly familiar.

'You're not going to shoot me, or you'd have done it before.'

'No,' said the speaking thug, giving him a tremendous welt across the face, 'but you'll still do as you're told.'

'Well, well, well – I've just been to a party,' Mado said, soothing his face and getting out of bed. 'You can't surely be asking me to another?'

None of them laughed. Perhaps only the man who spoke English understood what he was saying.

'Where are we going?'

'No questions.'

As he dressed and packed, he tried to think out a way of escape. He was no James Bond and he was well aware that if he did try to get away, they would shoot to maim. He decided to attempt a lighter touch.

'Oh! come on, sport, be civilized. I'm not resisting arrest. Help yourself to some scotch. I've been through all this before in Warsaw and Moscow.'

'No jokes, please. We know all that. Hurry up. Don't try and waste time.'

'Can't I leave a note for Matron?'

Mado was delighted to be instantly misunderstood.

'You have no matron, Mr Mado. We know all about you. You are divorced.'

'That's right, so I am. El Fatah's really in orbit these days.'

'We are not from El Fatah.'

'Right again. I didn't think you were.'

He received a blow in the back, which sent him reeling across the bed.

'I said, "No noise and no wasting time." Now listen carefully. When we are ready you will carry your bags downstairs and out through the entrance hall. The night porter will be asleep. There is a car outside. No calling out; no attempts to escape. Understand?'

'Yes, but you carry the bags. That is if you want me to walk out playing your game. Otherwise you'll have to carry me too.'

After a short, calculating look this appeared to make sense and an order in Russian to the other gorillas resulted. Then when he was ready they set off in single file down the stairs, two ahead of him and two behind. On reaching the hall, the night porter was, as forecast, asleep – or apparently so.

'Well, that's one way of getting out of a hotel without paying the bill,' Mado said cheerfully and shivered in the dawn air. He regretted not having the Swiss francs with him which Mournier had proffered a few hours ago. They might have been useful now. But that was already another life. He wondered where they were going to take him and what they intended doing, apart from freshening him up on Russian culture, of which he already had experience – as well they knew.

He did not have long to wait. As soon as the car started off, another car with diplomatic plates overtook it from behind and led the way to the docks. There was a momentary delay at the gates and then, as the diplomatic car was waved through, their own pressed in close, almost ramming the one ahead, and in a few seconds they were heading along the dockside to a cargo ship of about ten thousand tons which was obviously on the point of departure.

As soon as they reached the ship, Mado was hustled up the gangway and down to one of the crew cabins aft, over the screws. Then, securely locked in but without his bags, he was left on his own. A few minutes later, the ship sailed.

The calm of a British Embassy Sunday in Beirut was shattered by Padstow's saga, as it came to be known. In view of London's instructions he had been forced to take Mado's demand for money seriously. However, as the Duty Officer did not have access to the Embassy safe, Padstow had had to rout out Administration and then get authority countersigned by the Ambassador himself, who made the difficulties predictable in a high official disturbed out of his Sunday rest.

When eventually he got the hundred pounds in Lebanese money which was all that the particular regulations allowed, it was nearly midday. Padstow himself was in a rage. He had been at it since breakfast. The Duty Officer, Administration and the Ambassador himself had each reviled him in a separate and painful way. He was hot, frustrated and very angry with Mado. Whatever London might think, he was going to give that drunken sot a piece of his mind.

When he reached the hotel, the receptionist pretended not to understand. Padstow was told there was no George Mado staying in the hotel and there never had been.

'Nonsense. He's been here three weeks. Room No 11.'

'No 11 is occupid by a West German gentleman from Hamburg.'

'I was with him last night. I tell you he's in the hotel. Look, man, I'm not going to put up with idiocy of this sort. Where's the manager?'

'I'm afraid the manager isn't here today. Mr Hammamet is a Christian.'

'I don't care if he's a Seventh Day Bloody Adventist. I have got to see Mr Mado and I'm going to see him now.'

The receptionist shrugged his shoulders.

'I'm sorry, sir, there's no Mr Mado in the hotel.'

'I tell you I'm from the British Embassy.'

'Yes, sir,' the receptionist said politely, as if it took all sorts to make a world. Then he smiled at Padstow with that incomprehension which is part of the Arab charm, and waited for him to fade away.

'Give me the key to No 11. I'm not going to stand for this.'

'The room is occupied, sir.'

Getting further and further bogged down in Middle Eastern evasiveness Padstow began to feel more and more of a fool. He had a hundred pounds in his hand and no recipient to sign a receipt. Eventually he lost his temper. Pursued by an indignant receptionist, he marched up to room No 11 and burst inside. No 11 was indeed occupied by a West German gentleman, who was up to no good with a dark lady almost certainly not his wife. Padstow beat a hasty retreat, his ears ringing with Prussian invective, which luckily he did not understand.

He went back to the Embassy to try and think out what he should do. At his request Mrs Potts had abandoned her Sunday tennis and sat at her desk. But he regretted asking her to come in as all she did was sulk and suggest that Mado had holed up with a girl. It was one way of passing Sunday in Beirut, she said in a somewhat envious tone of voice.

Eventually, as none of his colleagues proved to be of the slightest help, Padstow checked with the police who in turn checked with Immigration. It was thus Sunday evening before the British Embassy knew for certain that George Mado had left the country in a Russian ship with the destination of Odessa.

The Lebanese authorities added for good measure that Mado's hotel bill had been properly settled and the misunderstanding with the receptionist earlier on had no doubt been caused by language difficulties. George Mado, they said, had left the country of his own accord. There was nothing suspicious in the official view. It might have been different, they implied, if he had been trying to reach Israel but the Soviet Union was a friendly power. If people wished to go to Russia, the Lebanese authorities were not going to stop them. In the meantime, the police informed him, the manager of Mado's hotel had complained officially at Mr Padstow's action in forcing his way into a guest's room that afternoon. They would be sending on a formal letter through the Ministry of Tourism to the British Ambassador.

To anyone accustomed to alcohol, the process of drying out is always depressing and painful. To Mado locked away in a tiny cabin without a porthole, hot, noisy and airless, this depression was compounded with a reawakening terror of once more finding himself in Russian hands. He had indeed been through it all before. He was surprised that they considered him worth all this trouble, although the act of brigandage by which they had got him was easy enough to accomplish in a town like Beirut.

But why? They had squeezed him dry once. How could the little he had learnt since his release be of use? In any case he was working in the specialized field of studentry and education. Things must be changing in the Kremlin if they were bothering with the young and the intellectuals these days.

So far as Mado knew, the Russian attitude to intellectual protest continued to be one of well-justified contempt based on the Khrushchev dictum that the Hungarian Revolution would never have got off the ground if a couple of writers had been shot in time. Although Khrushchev himself had gone the way of all good Communists, the Russians had been regularly cutting the intelligentsia down to size as they had done since the régime began.

No one talked to him on the boat. No one appeared to speak English. He was fed in his cabin, taken out to relieve himself if he banged long enough on the door, and allowed on deck for half an hour's exercise morning and evening under the unfriendly eye of a Russian quartermaster. During the early part of the voyage he had demanded to be taken to the Captain but the retort had always been a blunt '*Nyet*', so he spent most of the time lying on his bunk in his underwear, sweating and trying to work out how he came to be where he was.

He doubted it was Marides or his henchmen who had either double-crossed him or given him away. The motive was lacking. You could never be sure with any operator as rich and tricky as Marides – and Greek into the bargain – but if they had been prepared to pay him money and meet the conditions he demanded, why was he now a prisoner in a Soviet ship? Who else was in the know? That ass Padstow? His part in it could only have been indirect unless he knew very much more than he appeared to. Anna Novaček? She was capable of deluding them all but, cynical though he was, he was still reluctant to charge her up with this.

Perhaps it was Dinkworthy. Outwardly he had nothing to do with the outfit, but instinctively Mado knew that he must be connected. Remembering the look of the man and his reactions on the several occasions they had accidentally bumped into each other, Mado became increasingly sure that there was nothing genuinely accidental in Dinkworthy's behaviour nor in their meetings. It could be that Dinkworthy was the fifth or sixth man in his private mythology. Unfortunately he did not have one single piece of supporting evidence for this idea.

He was left with Ulf Achmed Azziz. The old Vulture and possibly Graziella, in her modest way, were the likeliest levers the KGB had pulled to get him where he was. Azziz knew – or strongly suspected – what he had really been up to. Mado had been very careful never to let Graziella connect him directly with the student activists he had been sent to contact, but Azziz undoubtedly had his ways of finding out any missing facts. Perhaps he had been stupid to refuse so abruptly a job pushing drugs for Azziz. He should have been less obvious. It was also inept of London to let him run out of money in the way he had.

But these questions were already academic. What was now urgent was to discover where he was going and why. He did not have long to wait. As soon as the ship arrived in Odessa, he was put under guard in an aircraft and flown straight to Moscow. A few hours after leaving the ship, he was in the Lubyanka prison which he had known with such dread a couple of yesterdays ago, as it now seemed to his steadily sinking mind. He derived no comfort at all from telling himself that this was where he'd come in. The main feature film was not necessarily going to be the same and, even if it was, the outlook could scarcely be worse.

'After all the consideration we gave that ageing chicken fancier,' Dinkworthy said to the Chief when they were next together at the club, 'he's done a Tarnham. He's defected.'

Sir Graham blinked but this was the only sign of surprise he gave.

'How many of your people does that affect?'

'Only Stevens, as far as I can see.' Dinkworthy paused. 'Of course, I don't know what he got up to in Beirut. I don't think it's very important. I don't know how much he really knew.'

'The Cabinet think Powder Train of growing importance. That's why I gave Mado another chance.'

'But he was going on to Hong Kong.'

'That was his idea,' Sir Graham said, a little testily. 'It was never mine.'

'And evidently one he abandoned himself without too much trouble.'

'I wonder what inducement they offered. It must have been considerable, after his previous experiences in Soviet Russia. I wouldn't put my head in the bear's den, having seen what the bear can do. He must be very brave or very desperate. Or both.'

The two men exchanged assessive, calculating looks. For all the surface bonhomie which higher civil servants are so practised in exchanging, neither really liked or trusted the other.

'We may know a little more when Mrs Tarnham comes back from Greece,' Dinkworthy said. 'She flew out yesterday with her children to have a holiday with Marides. We'll also see how things work out with Rupert Eynsham.'

'Ah! yes, the fourth man. Or is he supposed to be the fifth? I can never remember.' The Chief gave one of his mirthless laughs. 'It's about time the Press gave that one another run, isn't it?'

'It was also a fetish of Mado's,' Dinkworthy said. 'Actually it had become an obsession.'

'Perhaps Mrs Tarnham may give us the answer to that,' Sir Graham said, looking into the distance.

'Let's see first if she can winkle out Tarnham himself. We haven't told Eynsham she's going out to Greece but she's bound to bump into him. I've alerted the Ambassador – Jimmy Harborough.'

'But Harborough's coming back to London this afternoon for the Balkan conference.'

'I'd forgotten about that,' Dinkworthy said, a sudden look of fear in his eyes as if he'd been caught out. 'So Eynsham will be on his own. That should be interesting.'

He hesitated, and then said, 'Would you like me to go out for a couple of days?'

'Does Eynsham know you?'

'No.'

The Chief finished his brandy.

'I think it's probably better if you keep out of the way. Axley's on the ball, isn't he?'

'Our man in Athens? Yes. Axley in Athens and Padstow in Beirut are as bright as they come. Both are a hundred per cent so far as I am concerned.'

No wonder people took Dinkworthy at his face value, the Chief thought as he left. Dinkworthy made it very easy for them to look on him as a complete bloody fool. And maybe he was.

How long were they going to spend softening him up and for what purpose? Mado knew it all. The iron discipline, the filthily inadequate food, the interruption of sleep at unpredictable moments, the overhearing of torture in progress in nearby cells – all the varying factors of the KGB method had one object in view – the inducement in him of a state of despair. In his previous experience this had been to secure the confession they wanted for his trial. Now, Mado supposed, they could only be preparing some other trial – either a new one of his own or someone else's in which he was involved.

He was not interrogated. He was left entirely alone. The effect of this was simply and steadily to reduce him to a sub-human level for reasons he could not guess. His previous experience helped him survive but, as the days stretched into weeks, he knew the process was gaining on his inner resources.

His life now consisted of the cold, windowless cell with its bed of iron slats, its hard mattress, its one blanket and pillow, its table, stool and shelf on which reposed his tin mug and spoon. His clothes had been taken away and he now wore a vest, pants and prison dungarees with canvas boots, all of which were too big for him. For one hour a day he was taken up on the roof for exercise in a twelve-foot-square pen open to the sky but under the watchful eye of armed guards whose job was not only to prevent escape but also to ensure that he made no contact with prisoners in other pens on the roof.

Mado had always been a 'loner', a solitary man. He was thus better able now, as he had been before, to take solitary confinement. He had always relished his privacy and had long hardened himself to the nether side of loneliness. In late adolescence he had very nearly become a monk. Moreover, he had been through all this process before when there was every chance he would be taken out and shot. Now he presumed – though with dwindling hope – that sooner or later London would get him released. They had done so before. He was still a valuable man. When Powder Train had been mooted, it had obviously been essential for everyone, both inside and outside the service, to believe that he had been paid off and all connexions severed. As Mournier had put it, he was blown, out of work, drunk and lecherous, and that was the image it had been decided he should give.

The truth was that a man of his experience would always be connected for life, even though the use made of him steadily diminished.

But why was he here now in this evil Moscow prison? Why had it been worth their while to go to the trouble of kidnapping him in Beirut and bringing him here? What had really been behind the Marides-Mournier approach? Had it all been merely a part of the bait leading him into the trap into which he had now been driven? What had gone wrong? Or had they suddenly concluded that he would never have accepted an offer to work in Prague on the terms suggested? But perhaps he would have, after all, he meditated, and repeated the number Anna had given him as a sort of talisman – 258612 . . . 258612 . . .

7

Simon Dinkworthy was well aware that he was looked on by his colleagues as something of a good-natured fool. He had private means, he had been to the only school that mattered, his manner was easy, and he exhibited a non-patronizing, somewhat dated charm. In a sense he was a walking caricature of the well-bred Englishman who went out with Dornford Yates. It was a carefully fostered illusion.

In fact S.D. had a quietly vicious ruthlessness more appropriate to big business than to the higher reaches of the Ministry of Education. His ability was grounded in an acute knowledge of the regulations which he was at pains never to quote. He had a theologian's enjoyment of edging round a knotty point with an apparently impeccable paper argument. He was an Establishment man to such an extent that he could openly scoff at the foibles by which he lived. Whilst pretending to an elegant individuality, he detested men such as George Mado, whose singularity was real and whose value to the service was such that their independence had to be respected.

These traits in his character were so deeply buried that someone like Brewster MacFish, who was certainly no fool and with whom he had frequent dealings at Oxford, never suspected they were there at all. He saw Dinkworthy as an amiable ass holding down a Civil Service sinecure which must have been paralysingly boring. He thought, with some justification, that S.D.'s interest in the young had a homosexual basis, and as he had similar inclinations himself, he took care to protect this aspect of their relationship. Shrewd though he was, he never guessed that what Dinkworthy was really up to was recruiting.

Without knowing it, Brewster MacFish had long been a valuable contact to the Security Service in general and to Simon Dinkworthy in particular. All universities – and especially Oxford and Cambridge – attract such personalities operating on the fringe of higher education. Brewster MacFish, who had started as Bernard Greenberg in the Gorbals thirty-two years ago, had progressed from bad acting to the business side of the theatre and had then moved over to the exploitation of underground interests where he knew the money to be.

Apart from pop groups, his business ranged from fruit machines to the supply of special facilities for those whose tastes he had studied and who could afford to pay. He was not greedy, provided there was a reasonably quick profit to be seen. His contacts were impressive and, in spite of a waspish tongue, he was generally liked.

'I see you're still managing to keep the Wanderlust in the charts,' Dinkworthy said over a drink on his next visit to Oxford. 'How's young Philip Carlton making out?'

'Much better now that that hunk of Czech womanhood has removed to the Sorbonne.'

'You found Miss Novaček troublesome, did you?'

'Only because she pretended to be more interested in him than she was – or he in her.'

'Ah!' said Dinkworthy, as if this revealed a whole range of hidden truth. 'Ah! yes, I see what you mean.'

Brewster MacFish saw what Dinkworthy meant as well and quickly followed this up.

'Why not come along tonight and meet the dear boys?'

'Super,' said Dinkworthy, 'I look forward to the treat.'

Later that evening as he studied young Philip Carlton, he found it difficult to believe that this was George Mado's son. The good looks must surely have come from the mother. As soon as they got talking alone, which had been unobtrusively arranged, they discovered a rapport, but it was the rapport of two fencers meeting for the first time and suspecting that they were evenly matched.

'I think we did in fact meet briefly once before,' Dinkworthy said casually, 'but it was at a party and you wouldn't remember. You had some Bulgarian girl in tow, as far as I can recall.'

'Czechoslovakian actually. She was here for a term and now she's over in Paris helping to unseat de Gaulle.'

The student riots in Paris had just begun. It was May.

'You don't feel like going over there yourself to help?' Dinkworthy asked.

'Of course I do, but how can I? I have to take my degree. I don't want to be sent down at this stage of my life. I certainly *feel* like going. Who wouldn't? I mean just to have a go at those bloody Nazified flics for a start.'

'You feel intensely about freedom?'

'Somebody has to.'

'Does that extend to – to other countries? Or do you feel that's their affair?'

'Like Russia, you mean?'

'Now you've mentioned it – yes.'

'How can a liberal have frontiers? Of course, Russia is where the action should be but what can any of us do? There's always a Gerald Brooke languishing in some prison camp to remind us of what happens if you put a foot wrong in Russia.'

'There may be something you can do,' Dinkworthy said, watching his reaction. 'It depends on how anxious you are to help.'

'What are you asking me to do?'

'Nothing. I'm just sounding you out. If you would like to help, perhaps I could put you in touch with the right people.'

Dinkworthy found the young man looking at him curiously.

'You do know who my father is, don't you?'

'No,' Dinkworthy lied, 'I haven't a clue. Why? Does it

matter? Or are you saying he's some fearfully important nob?'

'I wouldn't describe him as that,' Philip said grimly. 'My father is George Mado, the celebrated spy, and we've just heard at home that he's now gone back into the cold – he's defected to Russia.'

'That's a rum thing to do.' Dinkworthy said. 'I gather you don't think much of your father.'

'You can say that again,' Philip said, 'and take your hand off my knee.'

'Ah!' said Dinkworthy allowing himself a sigh, 'I see what you mean.'

'But if the French are really starting something up, you can count me in.'

'Right, then, I'll be passing you on.'

Philip looked at him coldly.

'This isn't a blank cheque, you know. I want to know what I'm in for.'

'Of course, but you may not be what they're looking for at all – especially now you've mentioned your father. In any case, leave it to us.'

'I see. Don't ring us – we'll ring you, sort of thing?'

'Yes. I suppose you could put it that way.'

A number of facts became clear to Anna as *'les événements de mai'* began to develop. One was that she was not going to get much value out of the course at the Sorbonne for which she had enrolled. Another was that there was far more organization behind the rioting than people were generally led to believe. For every Cohn-Bendit who made the headlines, there were a dozen who quietly and effectively organized their individual cells, units or gangs – depending on the phraseology used – and gave the whole movement cohesion. Student power was coming of age.

She had been outside the university area when the barricades became effective and the Sorbonne was sealed off. However, constant communication *'par le talky-*

walky' had been organized. Two others of the Czech contingent were inside but their leader was outside in the same studio apartment as Anna. Surprisingly he turned out to be a young American called Saul Kretzer.

'You want to know who I am and why I come to be here,' he said to Anna at their first meeting. 'I'll tell you, doll. I'm that well-known 1968 figure – the Vietnam draft-evader. I carry two passports – an American one for going in one direction and a Czech one for going the other way.'

'How did you get a Czech passport in the first place?'

'That one you don't get answered,' he said, 'but don't let it worry you too much. My real scene is Prague and my telephone number—'

'Is 258612,' Anna put in.

'Right!' he said, 'and there will shortly be another number for us all to remember but this time in Moscow.'

After that neither asked any further questions and both accepted each other. Since leaving Prague at the beginning of the year, she had learnt not to be surprised, or at any rate not to show it. He gave her a letter from her mother which filled in the rest of the picture.

'If this situation in Paris develops,' Kretzer said, after she had read it, 'we think you might be more useful back in Prague, perhaps going on to Moscow. It depends how and when the Powder Train is ignited.'

It was then that she realized that the organization to which she belonged was on a far bigger scale than she had imagined. It was also apparent that, as were then taking place around them in Paris, unpredictable developments could race away with them all. You could only plan up to a certain point.

But where the roots of the organization were spreading in the soil, if you looked at it from one point of view, or where the buds were opening in the sunlight from another, were factors which up to now had been theoretical. That the intellectual ferment so wonderfully apparent in the West should or even could invade the prison states was now not only a possibility but appeared to be proceeding on an organized plan. Anna got higher on this than she had ever been on her few tentative experiences of pot. Her heart leapt every time she thought of it. The magnet of self-sacrifice was becoming especially strong.

Until now she had thought that only a few like-minded girls and boys of her age felt as strongly as she did. It was intoxicating to realize that she was now part of a much greater and growing whole. Whether this had been organized from the West or from inside Czechoslovakia did not matter. That it was alive and very active did.

'What has Marides got to do with it?' she asked Kretzer the day after they had identified each other.

'Money, mainly, why do you ask?'

'I saw you talking to his assistant – if that's what he is – when I went to get the coffee this morning.'

Kretzer did not hide his surprise.

'How do you know Jean-Pierre Mournier?' he asked, a new wariness in his voice.

'I don't. I've just met him, that's all. In Beirut.'

'Oh! yes, of course.' The relief in his voice made her suddenly suspicious. 'He gets around – that Mournier.'

'Do you trust him?'

Again there was a sharp look,

'I have to as things are. Would you trust his boss?'

'My father would.'

'Then do you trust your father?'

Anna sighed.

'Not so far as this is concerned. He's been an apparatchik for too long. Like his friend Novotny.'

'No one has Novotny for a friend these days.'

'And who was the other man, the tall, dark, English-looking one who was with you?'

'You ask too many questions.'

'I dare say. Who was he?'

Kretzer looked at her and paused. Then, as if he had decided something in his mind, he hedged a little longer.

'You would be very surprised if I told you.'

'I intend to know,' Anna said, 'so tell me. We have too much at risk.'

'That was Paul Tarnham, the English Foreign Office guy who defected three years ago. He's working in Prague these days.'

'But surely for the Russians?' Anna said, a growing anxiety in her vioce. 'Surely not for us?'

'That's what I'm not sure about. I don't know how much of Powder Train he knows. He's going back to Greece with Mournier. There's someone who interests them there.'

'Who?'

But Kretzer was not being pushed any further. He said sharply:

'Look, doll, I didn't ask them questions like that. You shouldn't either.'

'It's a good thing I do ... you want my real opinion of Mournier? He's a very dangerous man. I think he would kill.'

'I don't have doubts about that,' Kretzer said sombrely 'and you know so much – perhaps you can tell me what political change has ever taken place in the world without people getting killed? You think what's happening across there in the Sorbonne is kindergarten stuff? Do me a favour, doll, grow up, will you?'

She did not like Kretzer nor did she especially trust him. She wondered who paid him and how he managed to live. He had a Jewish-American aggressiveness, a somewhat transparent self-assurance, as she thought, which was certainly alive and attractive and yet in some way suspect. But then who was ever to be trusted? He had assumed she would sleep with him at their very first meeting and had not taken it well when she refused. Like Brewster MacFish, whom he resembled in many ways, he had a sharp tongue and an impatience, an intolerance which her Slav temperament found it difficult to accept.

But he also had energy. He was alert and he certainly seemed to know what he was doing.

In fact, Anna found herself lonelier in Paris than she had been anywhere else on this trip to the West. Perhaps because of what was taking place all around her at the time, she felt a cruelty, a violence and a bestiality in the air which had been totally lacking in Oxford. Police brutality, which she was seeing at first hand, inevitably produced a similar reaction on the other side of the barricades. She knew the Mao lot went in for torture to get what they wanted. At Oxford the feeling of being young and free had gone to her head but here in Paris she felt she had never been young the whole of her life.

Now it was she who needed a friend and no friend showed up. Then when she got Philip's letter, anxious about her safety, hoping she was all right in that decent English way which she found both touching and anachronistic, talking about the possibility of a European tour for the Wanderlust in the long vac and then adding as an afterthought, 'By the way we've just heard that my *marvellous* father has defected to the Russians – so that all this time he must have been a bloody double agent – typical of the bastard', she broke down and cried as she had not done for years.

So that was why she had not seen or heard of him since the Marides party in Beirut. She had been astonished at his sudden disappearance, expecting him somehow or other to get in touch with her during the remainder of her stay. Now she knew why. Now the confidence in each other, which she thought they had mutually established, the gesture of friendship she had made from her heart, even the Prague number she had given him as a token of trust – all that had been thrown into George Orwell's Memory Hole, like so much waste flushed down a drain.

She cried inconsolably and when Kretzer discovered her in this state, refused curtly to be comforted or even to hint at what it was all about. She felt a million years old and she hated George Mado with a violence surprising even to herself.

So her father was right after all, you couldn't trust the English. They would always be the smug, secure and cut-off hypocrites the rest of the world knew them to be. They were cut off in every sense from the Europe which she knew to be the only ghastly reality in the world. Her father had always maintained that Munich had shown up the English for what they were and they would do it again. Perhaps the French, whom she neither trusted nor liked, were right after all and perfidious was a truer adjective for Albion than even England's enemies intended. She had a childish longing to run away and be done with it all.

8

For George Mado the next move came as suddenly and unexpectedly as his kidnapping in Beirut. One morning, like any other and just when he had begun to lose count of how long he had been in prison, he was abruptly taken from his cell, ordered to shower, given a razor and some soap with which to shave and then, to his further astonishment, removed to another room in which his suit, shirt, tie, socks and shoes were laid out.

There was no sign of his suitcase or the rest of his things, nor was there a mirror, so that he could not see how he looked, but from the slackness of his trousers he must have lost a lot of weight. Perhaps today he was to go on trial or make a public appearance. Perhaps he was to be a witness at someone else's calvary. If this were so he was surprised that there had been no rehearsal. When he had been in the Russian power before, they had ceaselessly groomed and rehearsed him for those few hours of public self-denigration which their ludicrous trial system seemed to require.

Now feeling strangely ill-at-ease in his own clothes, he was curtly ordered to walk along endless corridors, up and down stairs, across courtyards and through some six or seven doors all of which had to be unlocked and then relocked after he and his guards had passed through. Then at last he found himself in a well-furnished office facing a tall, square-jawed, imposing man in civilian clothes who greeted him with a cold smile and indicated that he should seat himself on the other side of the desk. Mado did so and found himself being studied in silence. They were alone in the room. He wondered where the microphones were hidden.

'Well, Mr Mado, how nice of you to drop in.'

The English was excellent but there was a cruel twist to the mouth. It struck Mado that this one could be really mean without trying. 'I hope you have been well looked after in your stay so far.'

Mado said nothing. Previous experience had taught him never to react too soon. The other was evidently a little disappointed at not provoking a retort and continued to study Mado coldly and in silence.

'I am General Andrei Simonov,' the other said, taking a cigarette out of a box on the desk and then offering one to Mado. 'I know you of old but you do not know me. Won't you smoke?'

'No, thank you.'

'A glass of scotch perhaps?'

'It's unwise to drink on an empty stomach.'

'An empty stomach? Is the food in your hotel not to your satisfaction? Would you like me to have a word with Intourist about it?'

Mado managed a flicker of a smile.

'That should produce an interesting result.'

'Oh! yes. Yes, indeed. You can be sure of that.'

There was another silence. It crossed Mado's mind that the tape-recording of this interview would not be difficult to transcribe. He tried to guess again where the microphones were concealed.

'You seem to be puzzled, Mr Mado. If the accommodation at the National Hotel is not up to scratch, we must do something about it. Although I don't suppose you'll be there very long. You are staying at the National, are you not?'

This was said with an almost imperceptible nod. It occurred to Mado that perhaps the General was, unaccountably, 'playing to the micro'. He wondered why.

'You could put it that way.'

'I'm sorry our hospitality seems to be lacking in some way. I will come over with you after this meeting to inspect your room.'

'You do that, General. That should certainly cheer things up. If I can find my room, that is.'

Simonov gave him another chilly smile.

'I'm glad you're prepared to cooperate. That makes it unnecessary to go back into the past. Now we shall get down to business. Since you were last with us ...'

The General paused to give him the angry, burning look which goes down so well with the public at a trial, the look of power, the look of the slave master with the whip.

'... in circumstances we needn't recall, we've kept close track of you, Mr Mado. We thought you had learnt your lesson. We thought when we released you—'

'I was not released. I was exchanged.'

'We will not argue semantics. When we released you back to your own country, we naturally expected you to have nothing further to do with espionage. How stupid can you get?'

The General suddenly thumped the table violently with his fist. 'Are you never going to learn? I thought the English were meant to be intelligent, even Englishmen of Spanish origin such as yourself.'

Again he brought down his fist with a crash. It occurred to Mado that if the microphone happened to be under the desk, the vibration might well put it out of action. Could this possibly be what the General intended? He shot the idea out of his mind. There was no friendliness in those cold, hard eyes – only a look that Mado had come to know very well – the trained exhibition of ideological anger.

'Rest assured, my friend, we know everything about you. What you're up to, who runs you, where you gain useful facts and where you miss out. And I can also assure you that we are as interested in Operation Powder Train as your Chief is in London. We have a different point of view, that's all.'

Again General Simonov paused, doubtless to allow the effect of his last revelation to sink in.

'The code name of an operation isn't too difficult to obtain,' Mado said. 'What else do you know?'

Anger flashed up in the General's eyes.

'You do not ask the questions here. Do you not yet understand that we know everything? that we have complete control? that we know exactly what your instructions from Stevens were? that we have a résumé of everything you've put in so far? Do you not appreciate that the Soviet Union has the most powerful Intelligence organization in the world?'

'You organized four thugs to pick me up in Beirut. I think even poor old MI5 might have achieved a similar shabby little trick.'

The General banged down his fist again.

'You came here of your own accord.' Again the Russian gave an almost imperceptible nod. 'Your London masters know you defected. You were clever enough to leave a letter with Mr Azziz in Beirut which explained your real disgust with the fascist-capitalist society you have served up to now. This caused London pain and surprise but you are not exactly the first. After Philby, there was Tarnham.'

'Ah! yes, your actual Tarnham,' Mado put in. 'I was wondering when we'd get to that.'

He was gaining back his strength all the time. This interjection seemed to throw the General for a second or two and a puzzled look came into his eyes.

'What does that mean – "your actual Tarnham"—'

'You know everything,' Mado said, 'why don't you ask Alf Garnett?' Then seeing that the confusion was deepening and it was not to his advantage, he quickly added:

'All right – Philby, Tarnham – they're history.'

'But history in which you are very, very interested. Personally interested.'

'OK, sport, what am I doing here?'

The General ignored the familiarity.

'I believe you also know of Rupert Eynsham, currently

in Athens. Perhaps you may soon be adding him to your list.'

'Ah!' said Mado, 'that figures.'

'You see, Mr Mado, we know you inside out. We have studied what makes you tick and what it is you most want to know.'

'And you have the answer?'

He looked Simonov straight in the eyes. Again there was an almost undetectable nod. What was the General really trying to say?

'We are in daily touch. As we have been for years. As you so rightly suspected.'

'So what am I doing here?'

'You offered us your services. Like a number of your more intelligent colleagues you have seen the light – to use one of your Western religio-capitalist phrases. Naturally we had first to ensure that your offer was sincere, that you were genuinely motivated by ideological reasons.'

'And not just filthy lucre?'

'You're catching on, Mr Mado, you're catching on. That is why you've had a little delay in reaching me.'

'Ah!' said Mado with a smile, 'so that's what I've been having these last few weeks, is it? A little delay! So now you've checked up on me, where do we go from here?'

'You will resume your former identity. You will be working with someone you are shortly going to meet – in educational publishing – and you will be going to Prague.'

'On Operation Powder Train?'

'That's right. However, you will simply be reporting to a different control, that's all.'

The enormity of what he had just been told took a moment or two to sink in.

'And if I say no?'

General Simonov smiled with his twisted mouth, said nothing and then from a drawer in the desk produced Mado's passport.

'You are a competent, intelligent man.' He paused with the passport in his hand, looking at his victim. 'You drink too much and you have an unfortunate predilection for young girls but those are common faults. However, you must realize where you are. My advice is to proceed with the utmost care. You will make no attempt to contact the British Embassy in Prague. To try and return to the West would be fatal.'

'Then how am I to seem to be plausible? You said I was to resume my former identity.'

'That has been taken care of. London knows all about your defection. They do not expect you to contact the Padstow of Prague. I need hardly add that, if you do, I shall know right away and the consequences would not be pleasant. I'm sure you see the implications of what I am saying.'

'Oh! yes,' Mado said, 'I'm reading you loud and clear.' Then after a pause, he added. 'This is the moment for James Bond to burst into the room, isn't it?'

'Didn't you know James Bond is now working for the KGB?' the General said and for the first time smiled as if he meant it.

'A sense of humour is a terrible handicap,' Mado said. 'I think, perhaps, I will have a scotch after all.'

'I'm sorry, the scotch has run out. But I can offer you a good Russian vodka.'

Then with a deftness which would have done a West End barman credit he produced two glasses and a bottle of vodka from his desk and poured out the drinks.

'To the proper execution of Operation Powder Train,' said the General.

'Cheers,' said Mado, wondering how the first drink he had had in over six weeks would affect him. His previous experience of interrogation made him extremely wary of the blow-hot, blow-cold principle. He did not trust Simonov. He knew the vodka had been produced to make him relax, so instead he became more alert than ever. On the other hand, although they had him by the short and curlies, although he had no doubt that Simonov was strictly accurate in saying that if he tried to escape he would be killed, there was nevertheless something they wanted from him which had not yet been brought to light. What were they really after? What objective, human or otherwise, had they really in mind? Why had they gone to the trouble and expense of kidnapping him from Beirut?

'I can see you wish to ask questions,' Simonov said, refilling his glass. 'However, questions are not allowed at this early stage. Everything has to be earned. Later on, perhaps ...'

'I'm still reading you loud and clear.'

'Very well,' Simonov said, drinking his vodka in one gulp. 'Now I shall come with you to the National Hotel and investigate your complaint.'

The General was a swift mover. Telling Mado curtly to follow him, they left the office by an inner door which gave on to an unguarded – or apparently unguarded corridor – and then by a tortuous route which brought Gormenghast to mind and which, in spite of its secrecy. still necessitated the passing of four separate checkpoints, each guarded by an armed sentry, they found themselves outside the Kremlin walking briskly across Red Square in the early summer sunlight which was to Mado more intoxicating than the vodka he had just consumed.

When they were in the open, Simonov said:

'You are aware, no doubt, that we now have listening devices which can pick up a conversation in the open and apparently far from any buildings?'

Mado nodded. He observed that the General had blown his nose and now spoke with the handkerchief in front of his nose and mouth.

'I am going to trust you,' Simonov went on, 'surprising as that may seem. I shall shortly give you a document – similar to the one you asked for in Beirut. This will enable you to reach me personally whenever you wish but it is only to be used in emergency. Make no sign that you have received it, tell no one about it – no one at all

– and never leave it off your person. Stop and do up your shoelace if you have understood.'

Mado obeyed this instruction, causing them to stop in the middle of the square. By now the General had put away his handkerchief and looked irritated at this delay.

'You are obviously out of condition, Mr Mado,' he said, curtly and clearly. 'You drink too much. Over-indulgence in alcohol is a bourgeois habit I would advise you to lose.'

'OK, sport,' Mado said cheerfully. 'You're the boss. In any case that won't be difficult. You need money to buy alcohol and money seems to be what I don't have at present.'

'You will be given sufficient money for the requirements we have in mind,' Simonov said brusquely. 'Each according to his needs.'

'Ah! yes,' Mado agreed with a smile, 'I'd forgotten that part of the rubric.'

'In that case I would advise you to pull yourself together. Remember that you are still on trial – or perhaps probation would be a better word.'

By the time they reached the National Hotel, Mado was dizzy from the exercise, the vodka on top of malnutrition, the unexpected return to a partial freedom and the uncertainty which General Andrei Simonov engendered. He needed time to adjust. His astonishing new circumstances and the limitless danger in which he now stood, combined to put him on his guard to a degree he had not known since his last experience of Soviet Russia. There were obviously new factors to be considered. Things must have happened during his stay in prison about which he knew nothing. He would have to catch up very quickly indeed.

At the hotel the General was deferentially received and they were at once taken up to a room where Mado was pleased to find the rest of his clothes and his books.

As soon as they were inside the room. Simonov gave him a piece of paper which Mado quickly slipped in his breast pocket. Then the General said in his clear, angry voice:

'There is nothing wrong with this room. I can see no justification whatever for the complaint you made. I advise you, Mr Mado, not to waste people's time in this way. The matter is closed. Do you understand?'

'Yes, General, I understand.'

'You will shortly be meeting Dr Pivlik. He is a Czechoslovak educationalist, working in the same field as you. He will have expenses for you and you should do exactly as he says. Remember you will be under surveillance.'

'Great! I've enjoyed your traditional Soviet hospitality for the last six or seven weeks. Today I've had two vodkas and the big stick waved in my face. What about a carrot or two?'

'Convicted spies do not get incentives in any country in the world.'

'I was traded back, as you know, for one of yours. I'd already done a large part of my sentence. Yet here I am again.'

'Of your own free will,' the General put in quickly, 'which is why you are being treated in this way. Don't forget that. You must have come back to Russia with some purpose in mind. You tell me now that you are anxious to work for us. Why?'

'What's that?' Mado put in but the General was again playing to the micro and did not brook interruption.

'On the other hand how do we know we can trust you? That is why I am putting you under the close supervision of Dr Pivlik. If you do well, you may get your passport back, should you by then have any wish to return to the West. But I rather doubt you will. Once someone comes back here of their own free will, they rarely want to leave us, particularly when they have the opportunity – as you are now being given – of working to further the great ideas of Lenin.'

With a curt nod, the General abruptly left the room,

closing the door firmly behind him. Mado sat down on the bed and began to order his thoughts. He examined the piece of paper the General had given him. Although he immediately suspected it might be a fake leading him into another trap, he could see that it was apparently a KGB document of some authority. An up-to-date picture of himself was on it and the signature appeared to be that of Comrade Brezhnev. This almost made him laugh out loud. No wonder it was only to be used in emergency but what emergency was envisaged? Expert though he was in picking his way through Communist double talk, for the moment he found himself completely at a loss. Who was after what? and what was his role to be?

He began to examine his bags, packed so hurriedly in the night, a few million years ago. To his delight he discovered that nothing had been removed and there was even a flat half-bottle of whisky tucked in among his shirts. He poured himself a generous shot and suddenly did laugh out aloud. What would Padstow have said to this?

9

Dr Pivlik and the interpreter Borzonsky arrived a few minutes later. Dr Pivlik turned out to be a small dark man with sad Jewish eyes and an expressive mouth. Although he must have been in his sixties, he seemed on first meeting to be springy and alert. Mado took to him at once. Borzonsky, on the other hand, was young, shifty-eyed and sly. He had a small mean mouth, habitually stood with his hands behind his back in a sort of Russian 'at ease' position and had the misfortune to suffer from raging halitosis.

'Dr Pivlik speaks no English,' said Borzonsky, 'therefore I will assist you to communicate.'

'Great,' said Mado, exchanging a calculating look with Dr Pivlik. 'Was Dr Pivlik imprisoned at the time of the Slansky trial? I seem to remember the name.'

'The past is the past,' the interpreter said, 'we are concerned with the future.'

'Communication has got off to a good start,' Mado said. 'The immediate future might cheer up a little if we all had a drink. How about those expenses the big Chief talked about? Then we can get stuck into some vodka and find out what it's all about.'

The interpreter frowned.

'That will be attended to later,' he said stiffly.

'Oh! no, it won't,' Mado said, taking a quick risk and treating him to a burst of sudden anger. 'You have them in your pocket. Hand them over now.'

A flicker of shocked surprise crossed Borzonsky's face. He had no doubt been told to expect the meek obedience which Mado's time in the Lubyanka should have engendered.

'Come on, matey, give!' Mado went on sharply, 'or do we all go back to the Kremlin?'

There was a moment of stillness as Borzonsky made up his mind. Then, as nothing happened, Mado went to the door.

'Right,' he said. 'Out! both of you – and back I go to General Simonov.'

It did the trick. Reluctantly Borzonsky produced an envelope from his pocket containing a roll of roubles and a receipt.

'That's better,' Mado said. 'Now we understand each other, let's organize some of your lousy Russian room service and get down to it in earnest. I have a certain amount of leeway to make up.'

Looking back later on that initial meeting, Mado was surprised that he had had the presence of mind to back his instinct. He was making a quick recovery. He did not yet know where he stood, he lacked a number of essentials on which to make an assessment and therefore he would have to grope his way through a fog. He needed to catch up fast and there was no one to whom he could turn. But at least he was no longer in a small, evil-smelling cell in the Lubyanka prison.

It became obvious during his first few days in Moscow that General Simonov had not been exaggerating. They knew almost every detail of the work he had so far done on the Powder Train idea. There was now no doubt in his mind whatever that the fifth man – the sixth, seventh and eighth men indeed – were all in places in British intelligence, working as the Kremlin intended. They knew it all. Or rather – and this was important – they knew everything he had put in to Stevens in London. What else they implied and how this linked up with other material from other sources remained hidden to Mado. Nor did he very much care. What did it matter once the dyke had been breached? One Philby was enough.

Dr Pivlik had some general administrative charge over foreign students at Moscow University. Thus not only did he see them when they arrived and left, he had daily opportunities of contact whenever he wanted since every student facility required authority of some kind. In Russia everyone automatically clears any action, any permit with his next superior, before opening a door. There was thus a to-ing and fro-ing which exasperated the students, generated a vast amount of unnecessary work and provided Pivlik with a chance to check up on anyone or anything he wanted without drawing undue attention to himself.

In the first few days of his 'freedom', Mado sat in on Pivlik's curriculum, with Borzonsky watching them both, and had pointed out to him the foreign students who were thought to be of present or potential interest. This was done in such a way that Mado himself was neither observed by nor identified to the students being most closely watched.

'You will then do your calls as a specialist in English educational publishing,' Pivlik said, 'which explains your presence in Moscow, and you will afterwards be invited to certain parties. This will no doubt result in the private contacts we want you to make.'

'Not if I have this rancid character breathing down my neck all the time,' Mado said, pointing at his interpreter and forcing Borzonsky to translate it. Pivlik smiled.

'But you don't speak Russian.'

'Never mind. No one is going to trust me an inch if I go around with smelly breath always in attendance. However, who cares? I certainly don't.'

In point of fact Mado understood and spoke conversational Russian with reasonable fluency. He supposed that the KGB must be aware of this and had no doubt noted it somewhere on his records. But he had always kept this skill as secret as possible. When asked, he denied any knowledge of the language except the few prison words he had had to learn on his previous 'cultural trip'. It was therefore natural to have an interpreter with him, especially in these first few days when he was patently on trial. However, he intended to lose his keeper at the earliest opportunity.

He soon discovered that Czechoslovakia dominated the thoughts of the professors and students, the educationalists and the professional men and women amongst whom he now moved. This liberal escalation was what had taken place whilst he was in prison. Since very little seemed to get into the papers, the underground river of news about Czechoslovakia appeared to Mado to be impressively large.

As soon as he was identified as a visiting Englishman, even though obviously in the power of his interpreter, they talked to him in a way he found fresh and surprising. Even two years ago they would not have been talking like that. They still looked around carefully and still tended to cypher their thoughts into ironic jokes, but there was now a bubbling expectancy in the conversational air, a new surging of hope in the circles in which he now spent his days. Though nobody put it into words, Mado became very convinced that the idea of the Powder Train leading right into the heart of Russia was no idle dream. It could happen tomorrow.

He had still not worked out what was behind his being there at all, nor did he understand the extraordinary behaviour of General Simonov. Why had he been given this special emergency pass? Why did they pretend he had volunteered his services when they knew quite well they had abducted him? Was he in reality meant to check up on the weary Dr Pivlik, a man clearly broken to their purposes a long while ago?

Most nagging of all was the obvious impossibility of getting away. From Russia there could be no escape. But were they ever going to let him out to Czechoslovakia? Simonov had told him he would be going but each time he asked when, a smoke screen blew up through which nothing concrete could be seen.

But in Russia no course of action is ever direct. You banged on doors and applied pressure without apparent result. Then, when you least expected it, something would happen around the back. This was how he lost Borzonsky. Simonov sent for him suddenly one day.

'I hear you don't like your interpreter.'

'I don't think he has dainty personal habits. Why not get him some Amplex? Besides, how can I talk freely with Charlie always getting in my hair?'

'But you don't speak Russian.'

'A few words. I could get by.'

The General said something in rapid Russian to the effect that the identities of the fifth, sixth and seventh men in British Intelligence whom Mado wanted to discover were in a black notebook in the top right-hand drawer of his desk. Mado instinctively realized the trap. He kept his eyes on the General's face instead of looking to the right of his desk.

'What did I say?' said the General in English.

'I don't know. Something about the identity of interpreters being important.'

'No. I said an interpreter's life is not a happy one and you must have patience. You see you don't understand conversational Russian.'

Mado did not react. He was not going to give away the fact that he knew this was not at all what the General had said. Instead he simply kept on looking him in the face.

'The people I talk to don't speak as rapidly as that. If they do they are saying things they obviously don't want understood.'

'Exactly.' Simonov gave him a penetrating look and Mado wondered whose bluff was succeeding best. He did not have long to wait. Simonov opened the drawer and picked up a small black notebook.

'They're all in here, Mr Mado,' he said in English.

'Who are?' Mado said, without twitching a muscle.

'The names of our overseas friends. The ones you are anxious to find out.' He dropped the book into the drawer. 'Your knowledge of Russian is defective, Mr Mado. You need an interpreter and Borzonsky is a very good one.'

Then Mado found himself dismissed and taken back to his hotel. Borzonsky was indeed a very good interpreter. However, Mado never saw him again.

That evening he attended his first student party alone. Dr Pivlik who spoke French told him that Borzonsky was ill. To Mado's private amazement his passport was given him, 'in case you are stopped in the street for identity'. He wondered if Pivlik had any knowledge of the other document he carried around.

'When you get to the party, ask for David Brijoux-Schmidt. He is a French student. You will find him of help.'

'Is he my new keeper?' Mado asked but Pivlik merely smiled and said: 'We shall be going to Prague the day after tomorrow.'

The party was at the flat of Ivan Kholnikov whose father was high up in the Praesidium. Young Kholnikov was thus a member of what passes in Soviet Russia as the *jeunesse dorée*. The apartment was littered with Western consumer goods. There were stacks of long-playing records of current American musicals and British pop. Scotch was on offer and the host was attired in an outfit from the lower reaches of Carnaby Street. Even to Mado's experienced eye, the impression of being anywhere but in the centre of Moscow was startling.

David Brijoux-Schmidt turned out to be small, volatile and Jewish. He talked rapidly and there was a sharp humorous look in the eyes. He came at once to the point.

'Dr Pivlik told me you were coming. Well, we all know about Pivlik, don't we? His job is to spy on us for the KGB. So where do you stand in this?' and then as Mado looked round to see who could overhear them, Brijoux-Schmidt went on, 'The principal micro is over there in that corner. That's why the record-player is in that strange position: it helps drown the bugging.'

'It's a good question,' Mado said. 'I wish I could tell you. Or you me. You do know who I am?'

'Yes, I know who you are.'

They looked at each other speculatively.

'With your story,' Brijoux-Schmidt went on, 'the fact that you're back in Russia can only mean one thing, that you're here with the support of the KGB and therefore someone not to be trusted.'

'You'd be wise to assume that.'

'When was a student ever wise, Monsieur Mado? Moreover, things are happening so quickly these last few weeks that risks have to be taken. The Sorbonne taught us that.'

'So take a risk,' Mado said with a smile. 'All they can do is to shoot you.'

'No,' the young Frenchman said soberly, 'they can always torture us first. I was in Paris at the start of it all and I saw the way things can go wrong. When I got my visa for Russia, I was warned about you by a friend. In case I should meet you. You were described in strong negative terms.'

'Warned about me in Paris? Who in Paris knew I was here?'

'Your defection was a bitter disappointment to Anna Novaček. She told me she simply couldn't believe that you'd gone over to the enemy.' He paused and then added with a smile, 'Now that I've met you, I can't believe it either.'

'Good on you,' Mado said, 'you're certainly taking the risks. How was Anna?'

'Great. These are good times for the Czechs. They've suddenly let the sunshine in. In one sense Anna and her friends are leading the world – and they're very proud of it.'

He paused again, studying Mado's face.

'I take it you won't be reporting this part of our conversation to your new friends?'

'Let's get this straight,' Mado said tersely, 'I don't have new friends in the sense you mean. Only friends.'

'Then I'd better give you something you can report. To deflect their curiosity. There's a *petit voyou* over there in the corner who's due to leave the club – for not obeying the rules, you understand – come over and help me fix him. He knows Anna, too. He's an American draft-evader from Vietnam who operates on a Czech passport. His name is Saul Kretzer. And he is definitely in the pay of the KGB. I have some dirt on him you may care to make stick.'

The apartment was big and old and the room they were in slightly L-shaped. By this time there were close on a hundred people at the party, a large number in pseudo-hippie attire. All were drinking, dancing and smoking with a slightly self-conscious abandon. It was a bizarre comment on the power and protection enjoyed by these sons of the Soviet *élite*. Everything was great just so long as father held down the job. On the way over to meet Kretzer, Mado smiled wryly at the thought of what would happen so very quickly when papa fell.

As he went round the corner of the room, a familiar voice said:

'Good Lord love us, fancy meeting you here! Hubble bubble toil and trouble – *where* shall we two meet again?'

'Hallo, Dinkworthy, what are you up to in Moscow?' Mado looked round to introduce Brijoux-Schmidt but found he had slipped quickly away and was talking to a Chinese girl.

'The dear old Min of Ed Student Exchange Scheme – short title MESES – which some bright predecessor of mine foisted on us all. I help to keep it creaking along. What are you doing these days? Still flogging books?'

'That's the idea.'

'Let's see, where was it we met last time? Athens ... Cairo or Beirut?' Dinkworthy scratched his receding chin.

'I remember. It was at that Greek shipping man's party in Beirut and you were just going on to Hong Kong. Didn't come back on the Trans-Siberian Railway, did you? My father made that trip once back in the Twenties.'

'No,' Mado said. 'I didn't reach Moscow on any Trans-Siberian express.'

There was no stopping Dinkworthy once the chatter began. The memory of the last time they had met rose in Mado's mind and with it Anna's troubled face when she had said: 'I don't think you should trust him. I don't think he's a friend.' Why had she said that? What was it about Dinkworthy which made you want to sheer quickly away?

'I was in Oxford the other day and bumped into your son. He said he thought you were over here. Have you heard from him lately?'

'We don't correspond.'

'He seems to be doing rather well – and that pop group he's with – the Scatterbugs or something – I was told they're going to tour Eastern Europe in the long vac. Very enterprising these youngsters are getting nowadays, don't you think?' Then, without giving Mado a chance to reply, Dinkworthy looked at his watch and said:

'Well, I've another two parties to look in on this evening so I must be on my way. Moscow's very gay these days. It must be the wind blowing here from Czechoslovakia, don't you think? Lovely to see you again, old chap. Keep fit and chirpy, won't you?'

It was only when he met Saul Kretzer later on that Mado realized that this was the young man whom Dinkworthy had patted on the shoulder on his way to the door.

10

The encounter with Dinkworthy confirmed him as potential danger in Mado's mind. The gay fellow's appearances at Oxford, Beirut and now Moscow – though plausible – were altogether too coincidental. Mado had long distrusted and disliked him and now he put him high on his list of inside men. He still had no concrete evidence for this. It brought him no pleasure. In the dark watches of the night, though, it tempered an already steely determination to escape. That was the first thing he had to do.

How to do it was something else. He was in a trap inside a trap inside a trap. Trust the Russians to think up those dolls, he reflected, as he lay in bed beside Sonia, a live doll whom he had met at Kholnikov's party and who was obliging him on a temporary basis whilst her doctor husband was in Leningrad.

He had no doubt that Sonia was in the pay of the KGB since she had questioned him fairly acutely on thc people he had met at the party. But Mado had been at the game too long to let that worry him. Middle-class Russian scruples, tears and guilt all lay ahead for Sonia, but in the meantime he had this pleasant enough, dark-haired girl in his bed after months of enforced privation. Let the KGB take care of the guilt.

'You really came back to Russia to work for socialism,' Sonia said, 'after being imprisoned for spying? It's incredible. How do I know you're not still a spy?'

'You'll just have to work it out for yourself.'

'I see.'

She drew slightly away and looked at him.

'How else do you suppose I move about in this way? Your Gestapo isn't naïve, you know.'

'Don't call it the Gestapo. We are not revanchist Germans.'

'I beg your pardon. Are you proud of the KGB?'

'I'm not ashamed of it,' Sonia said. 'It is necessary for the progress and protection of the State.'

'It *is* the State,' Mado said, 'since everyone who is anyone is in it.'

'You think *I* work for them then?'

'I don't think at all when I'm in bed with a magnificent girl like you.' He turned and looked at her in the darkness with amusement. 'Now you tell me,' he said.

She tried a clumsy evasion.

'In London isn't it possible to belong to two clubs at once?'

'It depends on the clubs.'

'Well,' Sonia said, 'from all I've read about the West, I gather you can't change the rules of a club without joining it. Of course, in Russia such clubs are run by the State.'

Mado chuckled.

'You've got the double talk to a fine art. You should go far in the trade.'

'I don't think I like you very much,' Sonia said, abruptly changing her mood. 'It's time you went back to your hotel.'

'Great,' Mado said, getting out of bed and dressing with alacrity, 'and don't forget to say in your report how co-operative I am.'

They were waiting for him when he got back to his hotel. Two determined, brutal-looking men who ordered him to pack after taking away his passport, and who looked as if they would welcome the smallest excuse to adjust him physically if opportunity arose.

'Where is it this time?' Mado asked. 'Siberia?'

The two men did not reply but waited until he had packed and shut his bags. Then, after a careful inspection of the room, they led him to a waiting car. Several hours later he found himself in Prague.

'I was simply flabbergasted,' Dinkworthy told the Chief over their next brandy at the club. 'There he was cocky as ever at young Kholnikov's party, blandly going on as if he hadn't crossed over, as if he was still peddling school books to emergent countries. Of course I behaved as if nothing unusual had happened, as if it was the most natural thing in the world to come upon him unexpectedly at a private party for dissident liberals in Moscow – I even asked if he'd made his trip to Hong Kong and had arrived in Moscow via the Trans-Siberian Railway.'

'What did he say?'

'Said he hadn't arrived in Moscow by the Trans-Siberian Railway. By the way, he didn't make Hong Kong, did he?'

'You don't have to act the giddy goat with me, you know,' the Chief said with a curt smile.

'The point is what does Stevens do about him?'

Sir Graham Corby looked at Dinkworthy as if for once he had excelled even himself. What a monumental ass the man was.

'Short of going over himself and taking the rest of his department with him, what can Stevens do? Grin and bear it as he did when Tarnham went. It must be some consolation that George Mado may have seen the Red Star burning brightly in the East. He may have heard the call of the rouble but he's in considerably greater personal danger than he's ever been in his life before. They may have taken his offer of help at its face value but they can put him away for ever and a day whenever they choose. I don't know what made him do it but I wouldn't be in his shoes for a million dollars.'

'If we knew why people like Tarnham and Mado defected, we could shut up shop. Incidentally, talking of Tarnham, she and the children are with him in Prague.

The Chief raised his eyebrows and looked at his signet ring which seemed to be the limit of any surprise he ever showed.

'Elissa Tarnham?' he said. 'Well, well, well. So that's where she fetched up, did she?'

'At any rate, as we know, it's where Tarnham himself seems mostly to work from. He does move around a lot. He was in Paris in May. Our French friends cooperated as usual by letting us know six weeks after the event.'

'At least Tarnham didn't have the nerve to walk into the British Embassy in Paris as he did in Athens.'

'I don't think even Tarnham would do a thing like that.'

'I wish he had done,' Sir Graham said soberly. 'He made it very easy for us to know exactly what he was after in Athens.'

'You mean trying to get Eynsham into the net? He damn nearly succeeded.'

'Poor Eynsham,' Sir Graham said, looking into the distance, 'that suicide was a terrible admission of failure. Of course, he had just lost his wife.'

'And Elissa Tarnham was playing him up. She's really a first-class bitch.' Dinkworthy paused, wondering if this was the moment to get a plug in for his side of the house. 'I thought the Athens Embassy hushed things up very well. There's not been a word of Eynsham's suicide in the Press. It was a stroke of genius to get that Greek doctor to sign the death certificate as heart failure.'

'Who was your chap in Athens?'

'Stephen Axley. He did well but the work didn't seem to attract him much. Also he was trying to get off with Eynsham's secretary. Stevens thought it expedient to return him to regimental duty. I think he's been posted to Hong Kong.'

'Ah! yes.'

'By the way there's a vacancy in Prague. I thought that boy in Beirut was very bright. Young Mr Padstow. Stevens is transferring him to the Prague Embassy at the end of this month.'

'Yes,' said the Chief. 'Prague is where it's all happening

these days, I wonder how long the Russians will put up with it.'

'My guess is they'll never use force,' Dinkworthy said, 'not after Hungary. Those manoeuvres are simply a smoke screen. My bet is they'll have Dubček knocked off. If they put the tanks in, there couldn't be a better way of lighting the Powder Train, could there?'

'Hm!' said the Chief, 'I see what you mean.'

It would have been easy for Annabella Novaček to stay on in Paris when the riots came to an end. The course she was taking had been fragmented but all her friends were picking up the pieces and getting on with it again. This was her *annus mirabilis,* the first time in her life she had been abroad for more than a few days. Her father, her mother and her friends all urged her to get the most out of it she could. When the great exodus from Paris began on July 14th, she had been invited to go camping with friends in the South. But she was restless and this deep-seated tension in her grew for reasons she could not understand. By mid-July, when she should have been in the Pyrenees, she decided to go back home.

The sardonic Mr Kretzer went with her. In spite of an increased general wariness, she now trusted him more than she had at the start. Since their first meeting in Paris, Kretzer had been twice to Czechoslovakia and once to Moscow. By now there were a number of student friends of hers, such as David Brijoux-Schmidt, who were in strategic positions in Moscow and who were willing to light the Powder Train. Yet the more the organization grew – or what Anna knew of it – the more troubled she became at the dangers into which they were all of them plunging.

'Forget it,' Kretzer had told her when she brought her fears out into the open before going back to Prague. 'Where's the danger until something happens? It's when we get them out into the streets, like at the Sorbonne – that's when the danger begins.'

'It's OK to talk like this in Paris, it wouldn't be the same in Moscow. You know that.'

Kretzer had given her a calculating look. 'You're worried about your friend Mado, aren't you?' he said, 'and what he may have told the KGB.'

She trusted him least when he talked like this.

'My ex-friend,' she said.

'I met him in Moscow,' Kretzer said, 'at Kholnikov's.'

'How was he?' she asked and immediately regretted the eagerness with which she had spoken.

'He asked how you were.'

'And you don't think a man like that, knowing what he does, who goes back and works for the KGB – you don't think there's a danger to us all?'

'Look, doll, you don't really believe he went back of his own free will, do you? How naïve can you get? They took him back. He's a captive.'

'In that case the dangers are worse than ever.'

'Not when you know what they are. Ask yourself which side the Pied Piper was really on.' He gave her another shrewd look. 'He seemed to have lost a lot of weight but otherwise his tastes were the same.'

'How do you know that?' Anna said, a new area of uncertainty opening up in front of her. 'You'd never met him before.'

But Kretzer merely smiled and changed the subject.

July 1968 was a fateful month for Czechoslovakia. The background pressures were steadily increasing and though it was clearly to Russia's advantage to keep this hidden, the difficulties of doing so grew every day. This and the exploitation of some sizable contracts for the Middle East brought Panayotis Marides to Prague for the first time in six months.

'I'm in oil, shipping and background pressures myself,' he told reporters in Athens, 'so naturally I go where the action is. Which at this moment is Prague.'

No mention was made of the real reason for the visit –

the supply of arms to the Arab countries of the Middle East. He brought Jean-Pierre Mournier with him.

'My public relations consultant,' he said, when both of them were taken by Dr Novaček to meet the President, Mr Dubček and other members of the Czech Praesidium. What Marides never said was that his bodyguard always carried a gun. Also that a Czech alias had been carefully arranged for him in commendable secrecy, which was unknown to the Czech leadership of the day.

Once established at the Alcron Hotel, Marides summoned the world to himself in his usual way. He had in a high degree the power of the self-made millionaire to move around in a cosmos of his own, a cosmos which even in the Communist countries worked as a catalyst on the scene.

'Capitalists like me and the Communist *élite* are brothers under the skin,' Marides gave out. 'We're both of us interested in power. Only I have a hobby as well – the making of money.'

Dr Novaček, ex-Czech Ambassador to the Lebanon, and Paul Tarnham, ex-British Foreign Office in London, were both Marides men in their different ways in Prague. Each differed in basic outlook and neither trusted anyone at all. This suited Marides and made an instant appeal to his own Greek peasant mentality. Marides believed firmly in the right hand not knowing what the left was up to. Dr Novaček, for example, knew nothing of the organization to which his wife and daughter belonged, though this was inspired and paid for by Marides.

'Friendship and loyalty form a nice top dressing on business life,' Marides had once gone on record as saying after pulling off some particularly staggering business deal, 'but a healthy soil depends very largely on shit. Personally I've never been ashamed to admit it.'

Another of his attributes was to discover what people useful to him wanted for themselves and to see that they got it quickly and liberally whether it was money in a Swiss bank account or, in the case of Jean-Pierre Mournier, the occasional satisfying use of the gun he carried. Marides was no dog lover but he knew that if you want your house protected, you had better feed the animal yourself.

Feeding Paul Tarnham, on the other hand, was a tricky and dangerous operation. When putting the meat in the cage, you stood a good risk of having your hand bitten off. The greatest wariness was essential. Marides knew that Tarnham had defected for purely ideological reasons. He had a medieval religious outlook on the progress of the Communist ideal, which was proof against the normal corruptions Marides could offer. He was thus an extremely valuable man to the KGB.

Marides intended him to be equally useful to himself and with this end in view had engineered the attempt to get Rupert Eynsham into the net. Eynsham had been the Head of Tarnham's department in the Foreign Office and since the defection had held down the post of Number Two in the British Embassy in Athens. Marides knew that Eynsham had fallen in love with Elissa Tarnham, the wife whom Tarnham had coolly abandoned, so he asked Elissa and her two children to stay with him for a few days' holiday in Greece.

The attempt to barter Elissa as part of the deal for Eynsham had failed and, because Eynsham then knew more than was healthy, he had had to be silenced. This had been contrived to appear as suicide and it suited most interested parties to accept this neat disposal of the problem. Elissa and the children had joined Paul Tarnham in Prague and life in the British Embassy in Athens had then returned to normal.

Those were the bare facts of the situation in July 1968. Marides, however, believed in never negotiating except from a position of strength. He knew that to do business with czars and dictators you had to have something tangible to offer. He also sensed that the place to look for such an asset was in Soviet Russia's own backyard. Hence his interest in the Powder Train idea, and the Marides

Educational Foundation which was a convenient working cover for this development, under the nose of the KGB, of a counter-power which, if nothing else, would be a useful bargaining weapon.

The strategy and tactics of this were both highly dangerous. However, the stakes were considerable enough to attract Marides. No one, so far as he knew – and certainly no amateur – had taken on the KGB in this way before. A further attraction lay in the self-evident fact that if it did not work out as planned, or if he got bored with the whole idea, he could swiftly sell up and get out. There would always be room in Siberia for the wreckage inevitably left behind.

If, on the other hand, the process matured, there would then be no one in the world stronger than Panayotis Marides to do business with Soviet Russia. He had come a long way from that poverty-stricken village in the Pindus mountains where he had first boned up on the hard facts of life.

11

To begin with Mado was kept in a comfortless room in the Russian Embassy in Prague. Then, when more suitable keepers had been arranged, he was moved to a small hotel nearby from which escape looked impossible. They did not return him his passport and there were always two gorillas in attendance whenever he left the hotel.

'But you are free,' Dr Pivlik told him in that maddening double talk which he was compelled to accept. 'You may go where you like, just so long as you tell them first. In the meantime, here is your schedule for the next three days.' Dr Pivlik seemed twice the man he had been in Moscow.

It was obvious to Mado that they had foreseen and covered the possibility that he might make a dash for it. He was not to regain his passport. He hardly knew Prague and in any case were he to reach the British Embassy, he was now convinced that General Simonov had been speaking the truth and would be informed of this in a very short time. He had no illusions about what would then happen. They would get him in their own way and in their own time.

On the other hand he was also persuaded that there must be some dichotomy high up in the KGB which he had yet to understand. No trained Russian Intelligence officer of the standing of Simonov would have taken the risks he had with a man such as himself. There was now little doubt in his mind that the General was trying to set up a line of communication in secrecy. But with whom and what he was so dangerously attempting to say remained a mystery. Moreover, why had they sent him to Prague? To be a stool pigeon in sealed-off Russia was one thing: to circulate even to a limited extent in the free or freer air of Czechoslovakia was another.

Suddenly it became clear to him that, like it or not, deserve it or not, he must be under powerful protection. There was a fight going on of which he had accidentally – or by someone else's intent – become a part. This filled him with spirit, a great surge of unfocused hope took possession of him and his gambling instincts came alive.

This new feeling, which for the moment lulled his determination to escape, fed on the extraordinary vitality he sensed all around him in Prague in July 1968. What had happened to that brooding furtiveness which hangs over all Communist cities, chilling even the most committed of visitors? Where was the gloom? There was now a Western bustle, an openness, a sense of freedom in the air which Mado, who was more adept at taking the temperature than any reporter, found astonishing.

On his first day's experience it was evident that of the two gorillas assigned to take care of him, one was a Czech who acted as his interpreter and the other was a Russian in charge of them both. There was no love lost between them, a fact Mado noted for future use. On the second morning the Russian, who spoke very bad English, came into his room and told him that the interpreter he had had the day before was not available and that a replacement would be coming in half an hour.

'Then we'll get on without him. I've a busy day.'

'No. You will wait.'

'I'd better talk to Dr Pivlik.'

'No,' said the Russian, stony-faced as a dam. 'You will wait.'

Mado realized that this one, unlike Borzonsky, would not react to a display of bravado except perhaps with violence. He did not fancy a punch-up at that hour of the morning so, under the Russian's disapproving eye, he poured himself a restorative vodka and sat down to wait.

An hour later the man he had known in Beirut as Jean-Pierre Mournier walked through the door, gave

Mado an instantaneous look warning him to keep quiet and then announced himself as Mado's Czech interpreter for the day, backing this statement up with an official-looking document which seemed to have a visibly corrosive effect on the Russian.

'There has been a change of plan,' Mournier said curtly to Mado. 'Mr Marides is waiting to receive you at the Alcron Hotel. My name is Karel Zilina.' He bowed stiffly. 'Czech Ministry of Education, Department of Advanced Studies.'

They spoke very little on the way to the Alcron. The Russian guard was clearly in a vile temper and exuded a high suspicion of the new interpreter. To begin with, Karel Zilina pretended only to speak Czech and English, in both of which languages the Russian's performance was poor. Then as they swept into the hotel and along a lengthy corridor to Marides' suite, Zilina said sharply in faultless Russian that he and he alone was in charge of the Englishman and that when they reached the suite, the Russian would wait in the corridor. Mado could see that this went down like a double dose of salts.

'Get my passport off him,' Mado murmured as they went in, 'and it's game and set.'

'We have it already,' Zilina said out of the corner of his mouth.

Inside the room Dr Pivlik and Marides were sitting in adjacent chairs. The Russian had followed them in. He was evidently surprised at finding Dr Pivlik there.

'Ivan is proving troublesome,' Zilina said in French at which Dr Pivlik leapt to his feet and in angry, volatile Russian drove the guard backwards out of the room. After the door had closed, Dr Pivlik turned to Marides and said in French:

'He will need to have his mouth shut before he can report this little misunderstanding.'

Marides nodded at Zilina.

'Use the phone in the bedroom.'

Then turning to Mado, he extended his hand and waved him to a seat. Out of his pocket he produced Mado's passport and threw it across.

'You seem to attract a lot of trouble to yourself, Mr Mado,' he said with a smile. 'That document has cost me a great deal of money. What's more, passports these days are only of limited use. You need a Czech visa to be here at all. You'd like a drink, no doubt. I'm afraid I don't have the malt whisky you prefer but this is not Beirut.'

'I'll surprise you by saying no,' Mado said, putting his passport away in his pocket, 'but thank you for this.'

Strangely he felt more at risk than he had in Simonov's office.

'Well,' said Marides with that glistening Greek charm which Mado so strongly suspected, 'you were going to work for me in Beirut when something unexpected happened and you were no longer around. I was told you had "defected" of your own free will, which I found hard to believe.'

'You're on the ball there.'

'But it was plausibly put about and seems to have been accepted by your London office. This time they've written you off. This time there would have been no exchange. In fact – as I'm sure you realize – once the Russians had got you back, there was no reason at all to let you go. An extra billet in a Siberian camp is no great drain on the Soviet economy.'

'So why bother at all?' Mado said. 'You or the Russians or both of you together?'

'They only bothered, as you put it, because of me. I do a lot of business with them. I'm an extremely valuable person to the Kremlin,' Marides said, watching Mado closely. 'Don't try and work out where the microphone is hidden. I had them all removed. Human ones are better,' he added with a glance at Dr Pivlik, 'especially at a time like this in Czechoslovakia.'

'What are you trying to do? Run a miniature KGB yourself?'

Marides ignored the question.

'You may think I'm just a Greek bastard with too much money bragging his head off,' Marides went on, lighting a cigar. 'That's what the City of London often say and maybe it's true. However, I can do deals across frontiers which no one else in the world can complete. For this, of course, a number of independent sources of information – uncontaminated intelligence, I think your people call it – are essential. The best way of getting what you want in this world is to pay for it. As you know, I am a man of some little wealth.'

'That's right,' Mado said with a smile. 'They once said you could even buy up Texas.'

Marides gave one of those expressive Middle Eastern shrugs.

'No man bothers to buy what he already effectively possesses through other means. However, I'm not here to give you a free lecture on the mechanics of power.'

'Why are you here?' Mado said. 'More important still – why am I sitting here?'

The answer surprised even Mado.

'Because you are a man of integrity in a crucial place at a crucial time. Because I've invested money in you. Because you know things you haven't revealed either to the KGB or to your people in London. Because cynical though you like to imagine you are, patriotism is still not a dirty word to you.'

'You're wrong there, sport. Kitchener died in 1916.'

'And, finally, because in the world in which you have operated for most of your life, you have one or two private scores to settle which make sense to you and to you alone.'

'That's right,' Mado said, wondering if Marides knew about General Simonov's little black book and the *laissez-passer* he carried in his pocket. 'When I last saw you, your tame gorilla said you were having Mrs Tarnham out to stay with you in Greece.'

Marides smiled, got up out of his seat and went to the bedroom door.

'Come in and join us, Paul,' he said, leading Paul Tarnham into the room. 'I know you would like to have a few words with Mr Mado now that he's here.'

Paul Tarnham was a tall, dark arrogant-looking man with considerably more presence than his photographs had led Mado to believe. The 'Celebrated Defector' had a determined set to his head, a crisp, no-nonsense manner which struck Mado as the epitome of everything he most disliked in the English officer class. He wondered how the Russians put up with it but quickly reflected that, like the Germans, they instinctively respected the born slave master. There was nothing proletarian about Paul Tarnham. He was cool, patronizing and very sure of himself.

'How do you do, Mado?' he said, frowning slightly.

'Hallo.'

Each nodded curtly at the other, neither offering to shake hands. This confrontation evidently pleased Marides, who studied them both with a smile which Mado caught out of the corner of his eye. Marides was certainly enjoying himself. He reminded Mado of a cross-legged merchant in an Arab *souk*. The dark, hooded eyes, the apparent calm, the ability to talk and say nothing, the wary charm that waited for the buyer to make the first move – all the market-place attributes were there in Marides sitting in this hotel room in Prague, smoking his cigar and watching two of his employees sparring for position. Dr Pivlik, too, was concentrating intently.

'What can I do for you?' Tarnham said.

'I don't know,' Mado said grittily. 'You've already done enough for me as it is. I have to thank you for a lengthy experience of Russian prisons and the death of at least two of my friends.'

'I didn't blow you or any of your friends.'

'No? Then who did?'

'The people in London of course. You know that. They were always able to throw away any of us at any time.'

'And you had nothing to do with that?'

'Nothing at all.'

'Who did then?'

Tarnham shrugged his shoulders.

'How can I possibly answer that one? I didn't run the outfit. Maybe it was Eynsham. Or Stevens himself. It was nothing to do with me.'

Mado stared at him with cold distaste.

'And I think you're a liar,' he said.

Tarnham glanced at Marides.

'Is this all you asked me along to hear?'

Marides leaned forward to Mado.

'Cool it!' he said sharply. 'Like it or not you and Paul Tarnham are working together.'

'I don't think so,' Mado said, calmly looking Marides in the eyes.

'Don't you? Well, I do,' Marides replied with icy firmness, 'and that's what matters around here. After your recent experiences, I don't have to go through the threat bit, do I?'

'No,' Mado said, 'that you can take as read. I just don't like the smell of my stable companion, that's all.'

'Cut that out,' Marides said. 'You are working with Dr Pivlik so far as General Simonov is concerned.'

'And who are you working for?' Mado asked Tarnham. As always the answer was oblique.

'What Mr Marides means is that we are all of us concerned with the Powder Train idea but the motives are slightly different.'

The elegant, vaguely contemptuous tone of voice struck Mado as sandpapering a sore.

'You still talk like a Foreign Office spokesman. What does that mean?'

'Look ...' Tarnham appealed to Marides, but Mado thrust on in a rage,

'Whose bloody side are you on?'

'Let's not go back thirty years and talk about sides.'

'Listen, Tarnham, whether you betrayed us or not, you did defect and for that a number of your ex-colleagues paid a heavy price. I was one of them and I know. Now because of circumstances over which I have no control, Mr Marides tells me we're working together. I have a right to know what at . . .'

'So exercise your right,' Tarnham said, 'and see where it gets you.'

There was a pause as both men took measure of the impasse between them. Marides with his unfailing sense of timing, jumped in at this point. He addressed himself to Mado.

'Let me hoist this out of the personality area,' he began. 'There's not a lot of time. At this very moment Dubček and the President are trying to argue the Russians out of taking over the country by force. In other words, is liberalism to continue in Czechoslovakia or not? In that sense all of us here in this room are on the same side.'

'Are we?' Mado asked, staring hard at Tarnham.

'So this is the moment for all the preparatory work on Powder Train to be put together in one piece. The effective time to begin the process may be nearer than any of us think.'

'Except for General Simonov,' Mado said, still keeping up the pressure on Tarnham, 'to whom no doubt you report and whose interest is very much opposed to ours.'

'You're wrong in one detail, Mado,' Tarnham answered. 'I run my own show here. I don't report to General Simonov.'

'Now I know you're a liar,' Mado said.

'There seems to be no point in continuing this dialogue,' Tarnham remarked, and looked away into the distance.

'Paul isn't a liar,' Marides said with calm authority. 'He does run his own show here in Prague. Up to now – yes – for the benefit of the KGB.'

'But now he's defecting again, is he?' Mado said acidly. 'This time from the KGB.'

Tarnham drew himself up as if freeing himself from some slush into which he had accidentally stepped. He was certainly an impressive man.

'I don't have to account to you, Mado,' he said, 'but I will. I've been a lifelong Communist from the time I left school. From that I have never defected – to use your word – and I never will. I simply waited my time, as others have done before me. I chose my moment three years ago and here I am where I've always wanted to be. However, I'm no Stalinist. My sympathies are with the Czech experiment, which is why I am here now in this room, which is why I do not consider the Powder Train idea as being in any way disloyal to Communism or to Soviet Russia. Under proper control it could liberalize the scene in Russia in a miraculous way – but it must be under proper control. It is a power factor for achieving some necessary changes and that is all. London, however, as usual a good ten years behind the times, regards it simply as a plot to overthrow Communism in Mother Russia, which is typical of the wishful thinking, the dangerously inept, dated, amateur outlook of those who employed you in your shabby little espionage activities.'

'Great!' said Mado, thinking of the Lubyanka prison. 'That was a great little speech and it certainly puts me in my place. Where do we go from here?'

'I'll tell you,' Marides said, standing up. 'You're staying here. Paul and I go to Moscow on the afternoon plane. Between now and then we want some facts which we know you have. Why don't you go into the bedroom and talk to Jean-Pierre or Karel Zilina as we know him in Prague?'

'Why don't I do just that?' Mado answered easily. 'An order is an order is an order, however politely you phrase it.'

He glanced at Marides and matched his oily smile with

a glinting one of his own. His mind was suddenly clear and made up.

'There's just one thing I have to do first,' he went on, 'but that won't take more than a second or two.'

Then with a casualness he afterwards remembered with pleasure, he delivered the hardest punch he could manage into Tarnham's solar plexus, following this up with an upward hook to the jaw which sent him sprawling across the room.

'Thanks for bringing us together,' he said to Marides and nipped quickly out of the room. The Russian guard was nowhere to be seen.

12

His first thought was to get out and away. He raced along the corridor, not looking back to see if he were followed, and then took the wide staircase three steps at a time until he came within sight of the main hall, when he slowed down to a brisk walk. The desk appeared not to have been alerted and he moved quickly through the main vestibule towards the front doors.

As he drew near the door he caught sight of a group of three people making their way in. He turned quickly away, masking his face, losing agonizing seconds but fully aware that these were the last people he wished to bump into at a time like this. He watched the staircase down which he had come. No one seemed to be following him. Then, as the group reached the reception desk, he moved on quickly to the door and was out in the street, walking down as fast as he could without actually running towards the nearest tram in Wenceslas Square. Trams were anonymous and safe.

He swung aboard the tram, looking round to see if anyone was on his tail. He appeared to have got away with it so far. He relaxed, nursing his bruised left hand, and then tried to work out what Dinkworthy, his own son Philip and another fair-headed man were doing walking into the Alcron Hotel together. The encounter had been so sudden and the surprise so great that he could not be certain whether they had seen him or not. What were they doing in Prague? The crowded tram rumbled on as he tried to work things out. He needed to act very quickly indeed.

Back in the Alcron Hotel, the desk clerk was explaining to Dinkworthy and his party that Mr Marides was still engaged, would they mind waiting in the hall?

'Who was that man avoiding us seeing him just now?' Brewster MacFish asked. Dinkworthy gave a quick look at Mado's son and then answered vaguely:

'Just a chap I bump into from time to time. He's a publisher's representative, I think. Educational books.'

'I thought I'd seen him around Oxford.'

'He's my father,' Philip said, 'and he's working for the Russians.'

'Fancy!' said Brewster MacFish, as if commenting on the weather, but a little later he gave Dinkworthy a curious look. 'Seemed like he was in a hurry,' he said.

'He was embarrassed,' Philip said. 'We've never got on together since he walked out on Mother. He loathes me and I detest him.'

'You should have parents like mine,' said Brewster MacFish, 'who see you into an orphanage at birth and then leave you alone for ever.'

'There wasn't much difference,' Philip said, 'the way he treated my mother.'

Up in Marides' room Tarnham had left secretly with a possibly dislocated jaw. No one had attempted to follow Mado.

'He can't leave the country,' Dr Pivlik said,' his visa isn't in order.'

Marides laughed shortly.

'Visas don't stop a man like Mado. However, I agree. I don't think he'll go. He's got some unfinished business to transact. For that he needs us as much as we need him. It's a pity about Paul's jaw but at least Mado's got one thing out of his system.'

He turned to Mournier.

'Find him and get him back before Simonov does. Now let's deal with Mr Dinkworthy and his troubadours.'

Even under the liberal conditions of Prague in the early days of August 1968, Mado knew that unless he went quickly to ground it would not be long before the KGB or Marides, or both, found him again. He could not ride about on trams for ever. He considered going straight to the airport and trying to get on the next plane to London but then realized that visa trouble would hold him up if not make his departure by regular means impossible.

Perhaps he should seek asylum in the British Embassy right away. No doubt the KGB would be informed, and perhaps later on they would fix him as Simonov had threatened, but his life had been consistently at risk for so long that now, as he walked about Prague, this seemed hardly to matter. He had been on the run before. He knew what it was like and what roughly to expect. It held no terror for him. He had a lifetime's training behind him.

In Moscow things would have been different. But Prague was full of Western tourists. He attracted no particular attention. The specialists might be looking for him now, the general security police would not yet have been alerted. He still had a margin of time in which either to escape or go into hiding. It was then that he remembered Anna and the telephone number she had given him in Beirut. 258612. He had never written it down but he could remember even her tone of voice when she had told him the number.

A woman answered in Czech.

'Does anyone there speak English?' Mado asked.

'Who gave you this number and what do you want?'

'I need a little help and I don't like mentioning names on the telephone.'

There was a pause,

'Where are you?'

'In a bar on Zborovska near Vodni.'

'Go to the Vaclav Cidok Gallery on Vorsilska. You will be contacted beside the third picture on the left aisle. Identify yourself with this telephone number. Be there in an hour.'

'Can you make it sooner?'

There was another pause.

'All right. We'll do our best.'

The Cidok Gallery was more crowded than he had expected and the visitors all seemed to be young. He took up the position he had been told and looked around, feeling inexplicably relaxed and at home. There was no logical reason for this except that he noticed an alertness in the faces of the youngsters thronging the gallery. They paid scant attention to the pictures but a great deal to each other and he suddenly realized that he was present at some sort of forum or meeting place or club where groups formed and dispersed and then regrouped with animation and a brisk purpose in all they did.

Just as he had come to this conclusion and had begun to work out the implication, Anna entered, stopping dead when she saw him. For three or four seconds she stared straight at him in a hostile way and then turned back as if going out into the street. Galvanized by this Mado moved quickly across to intercept her and just caught her by the door.

'Anna,' he said, 'you came for me, didn't you? 258612.'

'I came for someone needing help. I had no idea it would be you.'

'Then why are you leaving?'

'I'm not going to help anyone to cut our throats.'

'I don't understand.'

'Oh! yes, you do,' she said fiercely. 'I trusted you – like a fool. Now even the telephone number will have to be changed. How could you?' she went on, and for one moment Mado thought she was going to break down and cry. 'We've enough double agents as it is.'

'I don't know what you're talking about.'

'Why did you do it? Did they pay you more?'

She looked splendidly fiery now that the anger was coming out. The sexual pull she had had for him in Oxford and Beirut seemed to have stepped up now to a much higher voltage.

'Why did I do what?'

'Defect. Work for the Russians.'

'Is that what you really believe?' Mado said. 'It's incredible. You couldn't think I'd go back to Russia of my own free will? From Beirut? You're out of your mind. I was kidnapped. Who told you I went of my own accord?'

'Philip. He got it from someone in British Intelligence.'

Suddenly it all became clear to Mado.

'Dinkworthy,' he said. 'Of course! That's who it is.' Then aware of Anna's troubled eyes on him, he went on:

'They're here in Prague.'

'I know,' Anna said, 'but how do you?'

'I bumped into them about two hours ago. I was running out of the Alcron as they came in. I'd just punched Tarnham on the nose.'

'You did? In the Alcron?'

'In Marides' room. They wanted me to tell them ... look, why are we standing here? Do you believe me or don't you?'

'I'm not sure,' Anna said, 'but I'll give you another chance. I've a car outside.'

Brewster MacFish and Panayotis Marides understood each other instantly. The orphan from the Gorbals and the Greek multi-millionaire had more in common despite the gap in age, nationality, wealth and achievement than Simon Dinkworthy with his Etonian internationalism or young Philip Carlton who had only been brought along because he was now the leader of the Wanderlust group and was George Mado's son.

'How many of these groups do you control?' Marides asked.

'Six or seven directly. And I can do a deal with three or four more.' This was a lie and Marides knew it. But he also knew that if MacFish saw the chance of a lucrative contract, he would make it his business to get the control he claimed. Money was the mainspring in both of them.

'And why have you come to see me?'

'I brought him along,' Dinkworthy said, 'because they'll

have exhausted their Czech and Hungarian dates by the end of next week. The Russian Embassy in London won't give them visas for Leningrad or Moscow. I thought the Marides Educational Foundation might bring its influence to bear.'

Marides looked at Philip Carlton and then at Brewster MacFish.

'So pop groups are now educational, are they?' he said, with a smile. 'I don't think you'd sell that idea to the Ford Foundation.'

'I might if I got just one Western group – and that from Oxford University – into Russia now.'

'And you think this is the sort of thing I could ask of Comrade Brezhnev when I see him tomorrow? You think at a time like this he's going to worry about a British pop group?'

'Not put like that, no, but he has only to say the word. And he might do it for you.'

'Well,' said Marides, 'I admire your nerve.'

'And I yours,' said Brewster MacFish. 'There's only a few hundred million dollars between us.'

'As of today,' Marides said with a smile and nodded their dismissal. 'Mr Dinkworthy, I'd like a word with you in private.'

She drove the car with determination and precision, in much the same way that she walked and talked. Mado watched her out of the corner of his eye, a strong, magnificent girl in a short dress of cornflower blue which set off her blonde hair. He wanted her very much.

'Where are you taking me?'

'Home.'

'What about your father?'

'Je m'en fouts de Papa,' she said, tossing her head. 'In any case he's not going to know until we decide to tell him.'

'Who's we?'

'My mother and I and the people I work with. Things

are very different in Prague since I left here in January.' She paused slightly. 'And *I've* learned a great deal. Where are your things?'

'At the Vodickova Hotel.'

'I'll have them picked up tomorrow.'

'And lead them straight to me? No, thank you very much. My clothes aren't important. I've lost everything before.'

'We're not that stupid. I tell you, things have changed around Prague. Once a police state liberalizes itself, as we've done here, what happens to underpaid informers now out of work? They've still got to live, haven't they? We simply turn them against their old employers. You've been in the spy game a long time, Giorgio – you know that.'

He laughed at her use of the name Giorgio.

'So you checked up on me with Graziella, did you?'

She looked at him with a slight frown.

'And not only with the girls you slept with in Beirut. You're a real rutty little bastard, aren't you?'

'I see your English is better than ever.'

'Yes. I now know what the feminine of twit really means.'

For a while she drove on in silence and then suddenly seemed to relax.

'It's a hot day. Wouldn't you like a swim? I know a marvellous place near the mountains. We can make it in an hour.'

'You're spoiling me, Anna. I'd love a swim. But it's up to you. You're the boss.'

'Just so long as you realize I am and we keep it that way.'

He made her stop on the way to buy bread and salami and a bottle of wine. It was time out – a gift – and he took it eagerly, feeling twenty years younger as they drove along the hot August roads. As if reading his thoughts, she said:

'It's time out for me, too.'

'You can have anything in this world,' Mado said, thinking of the Lubyanka prison, 'if you're prepared to pay for it.'

'Do you have a sense of Fate?' she asked later on.

'I used to. Nowadays I'm not so sure.'

'I have.'

'You're young,' he said, 'marvellously, beautifully young.'

'Why did you get into this at all? You didn't have to, did you?'

'It's a good question. I wasn't too hot at schoolmastering, you know.'

'Yes, I do know. Philip told me. Why does he hate you so much?'

'I was unkind to his bitch of a mother. I let him down. I'm not the right father for a good boy scout.'

'Well, I don't suppose my father would pass that test either.'

'Your father is an ambitious, old-style Communist. He's caught in the machine.'

'I'm a Communist, too, even if I'm not a member of the Party.'

'That's OK,' Mado said, 'I have friends who are Catholics.'

'Yes,' she remarked, as she parked the car on the edge of a pine forest, 'I can see where you might start to go wrong with women.'

'Let's try and find out where I go right with them first, shall we?'

They were quite alone. She led him for about a mile through the forest until they came upon a small lake, fed by a waterfall at one end. He was completely hooked on her effortless self-assurance, on her white, even teeth and the springy femininity of her walk.

'It's going to be cold,' she said, stripping off into a brown, glowing nakedness striped with white, 'but then that's what we want, isn't it?' She stood smiling at him before plunging in. 'I mean to come in from the cold, isn't it?'

Afterwards they made love with a fierce urgency which wiped out of his mind all the miseries of the last few months. Nothing for a while existed but the timeless present and that wonderful wordless beauty of knowing each other in the one way that makes the whole of the rest of life seem trivial, its efforts directed solely to achieving this infinitely small, infinitely big moment of bliss.

'You're just plain magnificent,' he said, burying his lips in her hair. 'Let's drown ourselves in the lake. Let's finish with it all.'

'I knew this would happen the moment I set eyes on you in that Oxford pub,' she murmured. 'It's funny how you know what it's all about in a split second but you still have to live it out.'

'Thank God,' he said, kissing her big breasts with the tiny, undeveloped nipples. 'Thank God for the living out bit.'

Then completely relaxed and exhausted, they slept in each other's arms in the hot sunlight.

13

She took him home that evening, first to meet her mother and then to be sheltered elsewhere. The Novačeks lived in some style as befitted a prominent member of the Party, married to one of Prague's leading actresses. Mado took to the mother at once. Physically she was a smaller edition of Anna but with more of a monkey face. She was quick and vivacious. A single look was enough to tell her the situation. Mado had expected opposition, resentment or trouble of some sort. Instead she nodded at her daughter and welcomed him with both hands. It was evident that mother and daughter had an excellent understanding of each other.

'I've heard a lot about you,' Ludmilla Novaček said in rapid French. 'Here you are at home. I think it would be wise to keep my husband out of this. He is a good man but it will only add to his troubles. I will go round by Maria's on my way to the theatre,' she went on, turning to her daughter. 'I know her spare room is available but as I am fairly well known, it's better if we're not seen together at this time. I don't have to explain, do I?'

She smiled at Mado, who felt alarmingly emotional. It was years since he had been moved by the kindness of strangers.

'It is I who should explain,' he said in his somewhat stilted French.

'There is no need. I know you are a brave man and a friend to us all and you are among friends. It looks as though we shall all need each other very soon. Your father has been approached by the Russians,' she continued to Anna, 'to help form a government in certain eventualities. This morning he refused, but the pressure is on. It is a bad time for him. He should never have left Beirut. He was too deeply involved with Novotny. However, there is no time for discussions of this kind. Give me ten minutes and if your father comes back in the meantime, make sure he doesn't see our visitor.'

Half an hour later he was installed in a box room in Maria Lidova's apartment in the centre of Prague. The Lidovas worked in television and were old friends of Ludmilla Novaček.

'You will be looked after here,' Anna told him, 'as if you were with me. But for the present we don't think you should leave the apartment. Will you give me your word? It would endanger us all.'

'You believe me again? You'll accept my word?'

'Things would be pretty black if I didn't, wouldn't they?' she said and gave him a memorable kiss.

Although he had only arrived in Prague a few days previously, Padstow already felt as if he had been there the whole of his working life.

'I thought Beirut was pretty bad,' he confided to Mrs Potts. 'Ha! it was a holiday compared with this.'

When he had been told of the appointment, he had not wanted Mrs Potts to come with him. The old bag had been at it too long. She knew too much and he especially resented the knowledge she had of his several mistakes in the Lebanon. She made him feel like a schoolboy. However, now that he seemed to be out of the frying-pan and into the fire, he was glad that London had insisted on her appointment. At least she knew the job inside out. Veronica Potts herself took it all blandly in her stride. The golden vista of superannuation lay only a few years ahead. Nothing in Prague or Beirut could ever be as important as that.

As soon as he got away from Marides, Dinkworthy had gone straight to the Embassy.

'Your chum Mado is here in Prague,' he told Padstow.

'That's all I need on a day like this.'

'If he shows up in the Embassy, let me know at once – and of course a top-priority telegram to London.'

'He's hardly likely to, is he? Any more than I'd expect to find Paul Tarnham sitting in that seat. I mean, if he is trying to be a double agent, he's not going to drop into the British Embassy and tell us all about it, is he?'

'I have the impression he's on the run. He might well ask for asylum.'

Padstow thought about it for a while.

'As he's still a British subject, we can hardly refuse it him, can we?'

'Just so long as I know the moment it happens. Is that clear?'

He had never seen Dinkworthy in such a state. The jolly Bertie Wooster façade had vanished and a kind of grey anxiety seemed to have taken its place. After he had gone, Padstow looked at his secretary.

'What's up with our educational friend?' he said. 'If I didn't know who he was I'd say he was on the run himself.'

'Probably just a hangover,' said Mrs Potts, busying herself with the filing. She knew a great deal about Simon Dinkworthy which she kept to herself.

'But why particularly has *he* got to be told if Mado appears? I know he's the travelling Inquisitor and all that, but why is George Mado so important to him now?'

'They've always entertained a cordial dislike of each other,' Mrs Potts said in the formal phraseology which furnished her mind.

'You mean they hate each other's guts.'

'If you care to put it that way – yes.'

'So you'd say he's gunning for Mado?'

'It wouldn't surprise me. They've both been at each other's throats for far too long.'

'Makes you think, doesn't it?' Padstow said, staring hard at the wall. 'Makes you bloody well think.'

As Anna had promised, Mado's things were duly retrieved from the Vodickova Hotel and during the next few days of enforced leisure he had time to put his thoughts in order. He regretted his impulse in bringing things to a climax by striking Tarnham. That had been a momentary and expensive folly.

On the other hand his personal and highly sophisticated knowledge of the Powder Train operation remained secretly hidden in his head. He was now fairly sure that Dinkworthy was the double agent he had been searching out since his first imprisonment in Russia. He did not trust Tarnham. He could no longer rely on Marides, whose interest in liberalism, he concluded, would only be developed to the point where it could be an effective bargaining counter in his business dealings with the Kremlin. There remained the mystery of General Simonov and the *laissez-passer* he had given him.

But Simonov had put him under Dr Pivlik's charge and there was Dr Pivlik sitting catlike in Marides' room at the Alcron Hotel. He decided that so far as he personally was concerned, it was checkmate – or at best stalemate until Czechoslovakia became really free. The pawns had saved him at the eleventh hour but Anna and her friends were still only pawns.

The moment he moved from the Lidovas' apartment, he would again be in acute danger – and what was worse, of no practical use. He concluded that the only sensible thing to do would be to get back to England as fast as he could.

'Leave us now?' Anna said. 'It's incredible.'

She was quick to anger and at moments like this Mado realized how insecure she really was. It also made her extremely desirable to him.

'Then you tell me what use I can be to anyone, shut up like this?'

He was cooped up in more senses than one. Although she saw him at least twice a day, she refused to go to bed with him in the Lidovas' apartment. Mado told her this proved how bourgeois she really was under the skin. She simply frowned and looked into the distance.

'You won't get anywhere by taunting me. This is my country and this apartment belongs to my mother's friends.'

'Oh! come on, you great gorgeous beast. I'm not asking your mother's friends: it's you I want.'

'Don't go on like that,' she said with sudden tenderness, touching his cheek. 'I know. I know how it is for you and for both of us. I want you too, Giorgio. Things are just not right for it now, that's all. It's not merely bourgeois prudery.'

'What is it then?'

'My damnable instinct, if you like. Whether you call it middle class or anything else.'

'Suppose you were to marry me, Anna?'

She became completely still, hardly appearing to breathe. She studied his face in silence, thinking at first that this might be just another of his bad English jokes.

'I know I'm old enough to be your father, etc, etc, etc. I drink to excess. I'll go to bed with anyone who attracts me – so sexual fidelity is out. I've made a howling failure of my first marriage. There would be no guarantee at all that the same thing wouldn't happen again. I've no prospects and no money. I seem to be generally useless even in my chosen profession. What better offer of marriage could you possibly receive?'

She went over and took him into her arms.

'You're a lovely man,' she said, gently kissing him, 'and if it comes to that about ten years younger than your son. But this just isn't the time, is it?'

'No,' said Mado, 'you're absolutely right,' and took her there and then on the floor of the box room which was now his home.

The next day she appeared beaming like a happy child.

'Here you are,' she said, giving him an identity card. 'Now you are a properly registered Czech citizen. How do you feel, Pavel Zdenek? Now you can move about Prague as of right. And I've got you a room of your own. It's in some student lodgings but the students are all on vacation. It's only temporary but it will do for the next few days.'

'Who fixed this up?'

'My mother. There are advantages in being married to an ex-Ambassador. Come on, we're moving now. The other piece of news for today is that Marides has got Philip and the Wanderlust visas for Russia. They went off this afternoon.'

He suddenly felt chilly in spite of the hot August day. Anna caught the look on his face.

'Don't worry,' she said. 'I know you don't trust Marides but there's no one else with the power.'

'Who have you been dealing with?'

'The man who called himself Jean-Pierre Mournier in Beirut and who seems to be Karel Zilina here in Prague.'

'Does he know where I am?'

'Oh! yes,' she said unhappily. 'I think he must always have known. He's running the whole of our side of things. I thought you were aware of that all along. Why are you so upset?'

'Nothing,' said Mado grimly, 'except that we're all of us in more danger of our lives than we ever have been yet.'

'Why?'

Mado paused, wondering how to put it with the impact which would bring it into a proper perspective.

'Have you had a good look at Mr Zilina?'

She gave him a curious, almost frightened look.

'Yes. What's so important about that?'

'Didn't you know you can always tell a killer by his eyes?'

Now it was her turn to pause.

'I've seen the same expression in your eyes,' she said, 'when you were talking about Paul Tarnham.'

Mado turned away and finished his packing.

'And you still think I'm a lovely man – ten years younger than my son?'

'We all do what we have to do,' she said simply. 'The difference between you and Zilina is that you wouldn't enjoy it.'

He looked at her in astonishment.

'To hell with enjoyment. Don't you understand that we're all expendable, then, in Zilina's eyes?'

'At a time like this, what else can any of us do?'

'You're an extraordinary girl and I love you, Anna. I'd like to marry you very much indeed.'

'I should be careful,' she said, 'I might just be after your money.'

So now he looked out on August in Prague from a rented room near to the University, wondering how long it would be before the KGB caught up with him, still unsure of what he should do. His instinct told him to leave it all and get back to England as soon as he could. If his son chose to wander about Eastern Europe and even risk penetrating Russia, that was his affair. If Anna, for whom he now felt a compelling need, chose to trust Marides, that was hers. She had saved him from a tricky situation, she evidently had powerful friends and they clearly wanted him to stick around Prague. This brought his thinking full circle to Operation Powder Train which, for all he knew, had already been ignited into its final stage. Ignited and no doubt carefully watched and controlled by Dinkworthy's friends in Russia.

He now felt he should check urgently with Stevens in London. Whatever the risk he had been far too long out of touch. There was only one place from which to do this securely, even if Simonov were subsequently to find out, as undoubtedly he would, and that was the British Embassy.

Once he went there, however, his precarious anonymity would be lost for ever. British Embassies in Eastern Europe are closely observed without and within by a variety of interested parties. He fancied he would get through all right. He did not anticipate the trouble he might have had in Moscow, for example, in physically reaching and entering the building. Prague was now an open, Westernized city. But the fact of his visit would certainly be known and that could well be a fatal step for him personally. He decided to spend one more night in 'free limbo' as he put it to himself. It was August 20th, 1968.

'You have a car,' he told Anna. 'Let's get out of Prague and have dinner in the country.'

'I was just going to suggest that myself,' she said with a smile which afterwards was to disturb him.

He felt more lighthearted than he had for years. He knew now that he loved her and, in spite of the vast gap in their ages, that he wanted to marry her if she would have him. The risk that she might say no, the fact that he had nothing to offer her except a battered will to survive, certainly no home, no money and totally negative material prospects – all these factors loomed as far greater threats in his mind to what he wanted to achieve than anything the KGB could throw at him here in Czechoslovakia. It was years since he wanted anyone, other than for temporary sexual jollification, in the shattering way he wanted Anna.

She drove the car with her feline smile, glancing at him from time to time.

'A decimal penny for them,' she said.

'I was thinking what an extraordinary thing life is and how impossible it is to express what you feel without being banal.'

'I don't find the way you make love banal,' she said.

'But it isn't just that, is it? You make me feel like a schoolboy when you say things in that way.'

'It's very important,' she said. 'The only life I've known has been so very temporary – I mean in all its good things.' She paused, staring ahead in thought. 'No – it isn't just that. If I only thought about sex, I'd never have come back to Czechoslovakia. I'd have stayed on in the West. I very nearly did.' She paused again. 'But there's something we have in common which drives us on. I suppose that's why we're sitting here now.'

'We can't win, you know.'

'Oh! yes, we can.'

'No, my sweet. Winning is for the Marides of this world. Not for people like us.'

'You're English. The English always win in the end. Then they throw it away. You're extraordinary, you English, the way you go on. England is still the only free country in the whole wide world. You live in heaven and none of you seem to know it. Why do you keep throwing it away?'

'If you mean empires – they're out of date.'

'Not to the Russians, they aren't. And I don't mean empires. It's the English values, I think, the way you behave as individual people. Christ!' she said with a touch of anger, 'you're still light years ahead. That's why you do what you do.'

'I'm just a common little spy,' Mado said wryly, 'at least that's what Philip thinks. I move about and have my being in the drains of the world.'

'What's so wrong with drains? Where would we be without them?'

'There are better surroundings.'

'Someone has to clean out the sewers – or we'll all rot to death.'

For a while they drove on in silence.

'I used to think I knew myself well,' Mado said, as they arrived at their destination, 'but the older I get the less I seem to know. Marides said something which surprised me, he said patriotism wasn't a dirty word to me. In its ordinary sense it certainly is – or I thought it was.'

'And then five minutes later you had a bash at Paul Tarnham,' Anna said with a smile. 'What was that, then? A passion for amateur boxing?'

'I didn't bash Tarnham for the Queen of England,'

Mado said, getting out of the car. 'He just happens to be a bastard who got me into a Russian jail and caused the death of my friends.'

'That's what I mean,' she said triumphantly. 'It's the English values coming out in a sanitary inspector. I wish we had them here.'

'What you seem to have here,' Mado remarked casually as they went into the restaurant, 'is rather a lot of military vehicles. I wonder why?'

The restaurant was in a converted mill and they had a table looking out on the stream. It was crowded but in spite of this it was almost ideal as a setting for seduction or a proposal of marriage. He wondered if this had been at the back of her mind as well.

'You've made me very, very happy, Anna,' he said. 'How about marrying your sanitary inspector? That way I can order champagne.'

'You're supposed to wait till the end of the meal,' she answered, putting her hand over his on the red check tablecloth, 'but in any case order the champagne.'

It was then that he caught sight of General Simonov dining with another man in the far corner of the room. The other man had his back to them but Mado's computer memory identified him straight away. It was Dinkworthy's friend from Beirut, the Prime Minister's personal troubleshooting adviser on delicate foreign affairs – Sir Graham Corby.

14

Mado's first reaction was to laugh outright.

'Did I say something funny?' Anna asked. She looked so happy, he hated breaking her mood.

'No, love, it's not you. I think I just caught sight of my death warrant, that's all. Sitting over there in the corner. The Almighty must have a great sense of humour. He's certainly timing things very prettily tonight.'

He told her who the two men were and then ordered the champagne, watching the peace and pleasure drain out of her face.

'And a bottle for the gentlemen in the corner over there,' he told the waiter, 'with my compliments.'

'No!' Anna put in urgently, 'no bravado. Maybe he hasn't seen you. Maybe we should get out now straight away.'

'You're joking, honey,' Mado said with an edge to his voice. 'He's seen me and I've seen him. Once there's an appointment in Samarra, that's it.'

She did not know the story so he had to explain. Somehow just talking helped to clear his thoughts. No *bono panico*. There was no point whatever in trying to run away. On the other hand she could just possibly be right. Simonov had looked at him without a trace of recognition in his eyes. Maybe that was merely the cat-and-mouse bit. He decided to put it to the test. Whilst continuing to talk to Anna, he took out the *laissez-passer* which Simonov had given him in Moscow and scratched his nose with it, watching for the General's reaction. It came immediately in the form of an almost imperceptible shake of the head. He smiled and put it away.

'All right, my darling,' he said to Anna, 'you can relax

for a while. The appointment seems to have been deferred.'

'I don't feel like eating now,' she said miserably, 'I'd just like to go.'

'And waste all this lovely champagne? Now I know you must be joking.'

'Please don't show off, Giorgio. I love you too much.'

Her composure was gone. She sat playing with her knife, looking down at the table and quietly crying.

'Well, that's one way of finding out. Don't cry, lover. This is just a part of the game.'

'It's not a game,' she said with a kind of low-voiced ferocity. 'It never has been and it never will be. Don't take these risks. I want you alive.'

'Keep your cool, baby. Lose your nerve at a time like this and we're really lost. Friend Simonov is on my side.'

'You're mad. Mad. Out of your mind. You've just told me who he is. You don't fool around with generals in the KGB.'

'I know that better than you, my darling,' he said gently, 'but don't stop trusting me now.'

'How can I trust you when you talk like this? The KGB is the KGB.'

'That's right,' he said, 'but you don't know what that document is which I had in my hand just now. Nobody knows but General Simonov and I. He gave it me himself in Moscow. And now I'm beginning to see why.'

'I'm going to be sick.'

'Oh! no, you're not,' he said firmly. 'You're going to drink your champagne and sit it out. For me. Because I'm asking you now.'

She continued to cry and stare hopelessly at the cloth.

'You said yourself we can't win. I didn't believe you then, but I do now.'

'I was talking about Marides. Maybe we won't win in the end – but we haven't lost yet. Here's the waiter with the food. Come on, sport, try for a smile.'

She shivered and seemed somehow to shake herself out of it.

'All right, I'll try. For you, Giorgio. After all it was my lecture about the English and their values, wasn't it, on the way out here?'

'That's my girl,' Mado said and poured out more champagne. 'There's nothing like a little raging folly to cement a new partnership.'

'I love you,' she said simply, 'and this may be partly my fault. God help us both.'

Although Mado had infused her with a temporary confidence he was far from relaxed himself. He awaited the next move, trying to work out its likeliest form. He decided that if Simonov left by himself he would get out quick. If Sir Graham Corby went first he would try and talk to Simonov. In the event they were joined by two other men, whom Mado judged to be Russian or Czech officers in civilian clothes. He watched to see if Simonov would point him out but this did not seem to happen.

'What did you mean – this might be partly your fault?' Mado asked and then with a gesture stopped her answering. Sir Graham Corby had got up and, after shaking hands with the other three, came over to their table. He bowed slightly to Anna.

'I'm sorry to interrupt a private party,' he said, 'but I wonder if you and I could have a word together, Mr Mado.'

For a second Mado hesitated, suspecting a trap. Then he said to Anna:

'Go and wait in the car. I'll join you there.'

She went without a word and Sir Graham sat down in her place.

'I hear you've been using your fists,' he said. 'I was also informed that you had returned to Russia of your own free will from Beirut. However, General Simonov tells me this wasn't so.'

Mado looked at him sardonically.

'How could anyone in London possibly believe a thing like that?'

'Because it was well planned and documented. Because you know how easy it is to change a man's credibility factor. Because, as you also know, you had been retired from the active side. I think you were headed for Hong Kong as a private individual, isn't that so?'

'I was still reporting in.'

'In commercial terms you were a seller but had no exclusive buying contract with us. That's why you were approached by Marides. That's why General Simonov's superiors acted as quickly as they did.'

'So why the great interest in me now? They grabbed me, gave me a nice time in prison and then sent me to work in Prague. Why? The Powder Train idea is a brilliant one but I don't know all that much about it – and everyone else in the world seems to know more about it than I do.'

'You don't pass on all you know,' Sir Graham said sharply, 'but does it not occur to you that you may be of interest for other reasons?'

'My beautiful brown eyes, you mean?'

'When you said to Tarnham—'

'How do you know what I said to Tarnham?'

'It shouldn't take you too long to work that one out,' Sir Graham said with the full Oxbridge disdain. 'When you said you supposed he reported to General Simonov, you were near the mark. In fact Tarnham is run by a rival section of the KGB. Had you accepted Marides' offer, this is where you'd have ended up. There is great jealousy between the two sections. You were, as I think you suspected, a stool pigeon.'

Mado's brain was racing to work out the permutations of the extraordinary information he had just been given.

'And Dr Pivlik?' he asked.

'He was one of the few links between the two sections. Dr Pivlik tried to be on all sides, as he has done his whole life. I should say as he did all his life.'

'Did?'

'He had a nasty accident last night. He fell from a fourth-floor window and was dead when they found him. A lot of Czechs fall from windows, if you read your history. It seems to be an occupational risk.'

Mado thought about the sad, dark eyes and the Moscow hotel room where they had first met. His uneasiness was growing all the time. He looked across at General Simonov still absorbed with his two companions and then back at Sir Graham, who was studying him with an almost malignant expression which reminded him unexpectedly of Jean-Pierre Mournier. He felt shivery cold.

'Why are you talking to me like this now?'

'Because you happened to come into this very unlikely restaurant tonight.'

There was a pause as Mado thought out the implications of this.

'And if I hadn't?'

Sir Graham shrugged his shoulders.

'If you could have got away, there would have been no further interest in you from our side and you might have made your trip to Hong Kong as an ordinary private individual.'

'*If* I could have got away?'

'Yes. Now you are more of a problem than ever to both Simonov and Marides.'

'No one is pushing me from a fourth-floor window,' Mado said, making a sign at the waiter to bring the bill. 'I'm simply getting out – now – while the going's good.'

'The Russians are invading in just over one hour's time,' Sir Graham said. 'They're taking over the country. You could have a much worse death than a fourth-floor window.'

'I don't intend to have any sort of death,' Mado said.

'No one in your position ever does.'

'You mean I know too much?'

Sir Graham did not reply. Mado paid the bill and stood up. Sir Graham made no move.

'Where do you think you're going?'

Mado suddenly realized that he might have to run for it again.

'I thought I'd welcome your Russian friends,' he said cheerfully. 'How are they coming – in farm carts and droshkys?'

'You make a mistake. They are not my friends.'

Mado thought about Anna waiting in the car. Whatever Sir Graham was trying to say to him, whether Simonov was working for him or he for Simonov no longer mattered. The only thing now was to get out.

'I'm flattered by all this attention from the top brass,' Mado said, 'but now I have to get back to Prague.'

'I'll give you a lift,' Sir Graham said. 'I have a car outside.'

'You forget I had a guest. She's waiting for me.'

Sir Graham smiled.

'Of course. I met her in Beirut. Her father will be a member of the new Government here when the Russians have disposed of Dubček and company. But I very much doubt if she's waiting for you outside.'

Mado darted to the door and out to the car park. There was no trace of Anna or the car. Cursing himself for allowing the trap to be sprung in this way, he searched the rest of the approaches to the mill and then went out in the road. It was dark and deserted. She had gone. He felt sick in the pit of his stomach. Sitting down on a tree stump, he lit a cigarette and tried to order his thoughts. He could not believe she had gone of her own free will. If she, too, was treacherous then there was really no hope. But if she had been seized and forced to drive away, then their visit to the mill that evening could not have been the accident he had imagined it was. She had brought him there deliberately – possibly without knowing why.

As he walked back to the restaurant door, Sir Graham Corby came out.

'You were right,' Mado said. 'I'd like to accept your offer of a lift.'

Sir Graham drove fast and well. There seemed to be unusually little traffic about and Mado's sense of foreboding grew. For a while they drove in silence. Mado covertly examined the Chief in whose hands his fate now seemed to lie, as it must have done many times in the past without his knowing.

'You didn't know I was coming to that restaurant tonight?' Mado asked after a while.

'Neither did General Simonov.'

'Yet you guessed Miss Novaček would have gone ...'

'Not a very difficult deduction. Your visit to the mill was either pure coincidence or the Marides-Tarnham faction thought they would fix both of you that way – so her part of the job was done.'

'Fix both of us? Why should Marides want to do that? Anna was working for him anyway and I was "under offer" so to speak.'

'You hadn't exactly accepted, had you? Unless punching Tarnham on the nose is your way of signing a contract.'

'I still don't get the motive,' Mado said. He did not trust this sombre-looking man with the calculating eyes. 'Look, I know you and I are not on the same level of activity—'

Sir Graham interrupted him almost impatiently.

'The most likely thing is that they wanted to kill two birds with one stone – expose you to the man from whom you had escaped, and do a little horse-trading with Novaček's daughter.'

'You mean she's a hostage for her father?'

'Wouldn't you take a precaution of that kind if you were trying to set up a puppet government in Czechoslovakia today?'

'It seems a bit too coincidental to me. Suppose you hadn't been there? Suppose you hadn't come over to talk to me?'

'I don't think there was anything coincidental about your arrival at that restaurant tonight. I'd say it was carefully planned. They were not primarily concerned with you. It was the girl they were after. I expect they made her think the heat was on you – and that's why she cooperated as she did. She expected to find one of Marides' group at the mill.'

'But I suggested a dinner out of town myself.'

Sir Graham gave a twitch of a smile and continued to drive on in silence. Then, after allowing time for the implications to sink in, he said quietly:

'She's young but she's nevertheless a well-trained agent.'

'Who sold you that idea?' Mado said sourly. But a seed of doubt had sprung to life in his mind and he felt suddenly sick.

'No one sells me ideas of that kind,' Sir Graham said coldly, leaving the enigma where it was. Mado had the impression that the Chief was looking down on him from a height and found him a colossal bore. But what had he been doing with Simonov?

By now they were on the outskirts of Prague. Mado had fallen silent trying to work it all out. There were a number of questions he wanted to ask but experience told him that Sir Graham Corby was extremely unlikely to answer them. Moreover, his instinct was working overtime. He began to force his thoughts to swim against the stream of events. Why, for instance, had General Simonov shaken his head on seeing the *laissez-passer* he had given Mado? What exactly was the General's position?

They reached the approach to the British Embassy and were stopped by the Czech security police.

'Show your British passport,' said Sir Graham curtly, as if he knew that Mado also had Czech papers. A few moments later they were allowed through. As they walked up the Embassy steps, Mado decided to risk a key question.

'Has General Simonov defected?' he asked.

'I don't think that is the word for General Simonov,' Sir Graham said. 'I know him well but I don't think he has the inclination or the intention of removing himself physically to the West. I doubt, though, that that is the sort of thing it would be politic to ask him in Moscow. He told me he was returning there tomorrow, when the invasion has taken place.'

As they entered the hall of the Embassy, Padstow appeared. He was unable to conceal his surprise at seeing Mado with Sir Graham Corby but this was only a momentary flash.

'The Ambassador will see you at once, Sir Graham,' he said and led him away, leaving Mado alone with the security guard in the hall. He decided to wait until Padstow reappeared and then play it by ear. He was in possession of a number of highly explosive facts and although neither Simonov nor Corby had appeared in any way disturbed at his presence, he sensed that his life could well be in danger from both of them. He lit a cigarette and waited for young Mr Padstow to reappear.

15

The night the Russians invaded Czechoslovakia became for Padstow the most extraordinary he had yet experienced in his service career. To begin with his private judgement had again been proved wrong and the bets he had taken on non-intervention forfeit. Then as the night wore on, there was this objectionable little man calling him 'sport' and sitting in his office as if he owned it.

'I suppose I really ought to arrest you,' he said. 'After all, you did defect on active service, so to speak.'

Mado looked at him wryly and then laughed.

'Well, thank God you're still around for the light relief.'

'But you did, didn't you? I saw the letter you left in your own handwriting with Ulf Achmed Azziz.'

'Did you ever know my handwriting?'

'Not really. I did know your signature. The whole thing looked genuine.'

'It would have to, wouldn't it?' Mado said sharply. This was all a great waste of valuable time. He decided to press on.

'Then you'll have to ask yourself if I'm merely defecting back again. You'll need a computer to keep up with it all.'

'Apart from sending me up and making a complete fool of me in Beirut, what can I do for you?'

Mado stared at him, trying to assess the young man's quality through the layers of convention which had been applied on top. There might be a shaft of truth in him, if he took the trouble to find it. It might well be worth the risk and the effort. He drew a bow at a venture.

'I'll startle you with a little second sight,' he said, 'and you can tell me if I'm right. Simon Dinkworthy has been to see you in the last couple of days. He warned you I was here in Prague and asked you to let him know when I showed up.'

He could tell he had scored a hit from the startled look on Padstow's face. There was a long pause.

'I don't see that Dinkworthy has anything to do with it.'

'Exactly. He's in Education – as I am.'

'What are you proposing to do?' Padstow asked in a much less aggressive way. 'What do you want to do?'

'Communicate with someone I can trust. And I know that this is scarcely the night.'

Padstow looked at him reflectively.

'Perhaps London will communicate with you. I've already sent off a telegram telling them you're here.'

Mado smiled.

'I believe I could be winning the battle for Padstow, couldn't I?'

'I don't know what that means but—'

'I need someone I can rely on, Mr Padstow. Let's say I'm rather badly in need of a friend. They're in short supply around Prague these days.'

They looked at each other, each in his own thoughts assessing and calculating.

'What made you go in for this fancy line of work?' Mado asked eventually.

'Father was an admiral, both my grandfathers were generals but I didn't want to go into the Navy, the Army or the Air Force and there was no Indian Civil Service when I came along. What do you do if you're still old-fashioned enough to want to serve your country?' He shrugged his shoulders. 'It's not what I thought it would be.'

'What would you do if you discovered your Ambassador fiddling the petty cash in a big way?'

Padstow's answer gave Mado his second laugh that evening.

'I don't know. Go to the Queen, I suppose. My father knows people in the Household.'

'You mean it always pays to go to the top?'

'Yes,' Padstow said in all seriousness, 'at least you know where you are.'

'I suppose it's her country we're all trying to preserve or defect from or whatever it is we're up to.'

'Yes.'

'You wouldn't try the Head of the Foreign Service or someone further up the line?'

Padstow stared at him hard before answering and then Mado knew he had his man.

'I've only been in this outfit a short time, but I'll say this. From the way I've seen the Establishment bend its own regulations to suit its own particular purposes, I'd rather trust a second-hand car salesman in Bethnal Green.'

'But the British Civil Service is the envy of the world.'

'No,' Padstow said acidly, 'they only envy themselves. They believe they're impeccable. They relish – no, that's the wrong word – they wallow in their power. They really believe their own double talk whereas in private they're mean, ambitious and spiteful. And some of them are bent.'

Mado was astonished at the violence he had accidentally uncovered.

'Are you saying that all our lovely higher civil servants lack integrity?'

'Well, I don't see much of it about, do you? They're all out for themselves and the regulations are framed with that end in view. You yourself said in Beirut that Philby couldn't possibly have operated for thirty years alone.'

'Now you're getting warm.'

'Then there was Tarnham. There must still be others – snug as little worms eating into the rotten biscuit.'

'You're right on beam,' Mado said with pleasure at the way life suddenly adjusted the odds at the unlikeliest moment.

'Of course, I only see a very small part of the parish.

And so far as Dinkworthy is concerned, I don't happen to be queer. He told me he'd put in a good word for me in getting this appointment. I don't know if he was making a pass at me in a subtle way. Maybe he thinks I'm just a public-school nit.'

'Right, Mr Padstow, you've really got the message. Second question – what would you do if you were me? Now – on a night like this?'

'I'd get the hell out of it back to London as fast as I could.'

'And see the Queen?'

'And see the Queen.'

'Yes,' said Mado, 'the snag is to get the proof I need. It's no good going without the proof. And Moscow is where it will be.'

There was a lengthy pause as they studied each other. Mado was smiling and Padstow, to his great surprise, found himself admiring the man.

'You're mad,' Padstow said. 'You'll never make it. Not in a million years.'

'You're the second person tonight who's called me mad. And she's disappeared.'

He produced his *laissez-passer* and showed it to Padstow.

'You're the only other person to have seen that document,' he said, 'and that shows you how mad I am. And do you know who was dining with Sir Graham Corby tonight? General Simonov of the KGB.'

'Well,' Padstow said after he had thought out the extraordinary implications of the extraordinary facts he had just been told, 'I'm only a very small cog in this lousy machine – but this office is yours and any help I can give you.'

'Thanks,' Mado said, 'I don't think Whitehall will be recommending you for the OBE.'

He dozed in a chair in Padstow's office. Throughout the night he tried at intervals to phone Anna's home but the line was always engaged or out of order. As the night went through, there was increasing activity around him in the Embassy while the appalling gravity of the situation came into focus. By the time Prague busied itself into life in the morning, dozens of Russian tanks were in positions of control, the Czech leaders had been abducted to Russia, manacled like common criminals, and the occupation was a fact in the history of the world.

As soon as he could move about without attracting attention, he made his way to the Lidovas' apartment and a few minutes later Anna's mother arrived with the anguishing news that Anna had not shown up all night nor had there been a phone call.

'What about your husband? Is he going in with the Russians?'

'No.' Ludmilla Novaček was obviously in a state of near collapse. 'He has decided to do nothing, though his sympathies are not with Dubček. He is trying to find out where Anna is through his Russian contacts. I think they will get him to Moscow.'

He told her exactly what had happened at the mill.

'She was crazy to take you to that place. The Gestapo used it in the war: it's the sort of place the KGB would pick for a temporary headquarters.'

'Could she still be there? The car was gone.'

'I don't think so. They would want the place for other things.'

'Why did she take me there?'

'I don't really know. I think the man who calls himself Karel Zilina intended meeting you there but something went wrong. Marides has gone and so has Zilina. Something happened when Dr Pivlik was murdered. Anyway, now the Russians are here, it's clear we've been abandoned again. We Czechs are used to being on our own.'

They looked at each other in lively understanding of the danger, the anxiety and the real confusion in which both of them stood. The gap of language, civilization, background and sex seemed to have narrowed to an almost invisible point. Instinctively he took her hand.

'You're a very remarkable woman,' Mado said, 'and this is a time above all to keep the faith. Where do you think she is?'

'I'm afraid they will have taken her to Russia. So far as my husband is concerned, she is a valuable hostage.' She paused for a moment and then added, 'Your son is in Russia, too.'

'Is there anything your husband can do now – at this moment?'

'What can any of us do at a time like this? Somehow or other we have got to survive. We are all of us marked.'

'Well,' Mado said with a grim smile, 'I'm no St George but I know the Dragon I'm after.'

'I think you would be wise to go back to London just as soon as you can. Who knows when the frontiers will close?'

'Yes,' Mado said, 'that would be the wise thing to do.'

He returned to the British Embassy past the tanks with swastikas daubed on their sides, past groups of puzzled Russian soldiers trying to comprehend the 'welcome' they had been given, past Czech security guards who seemed stunned into apathy. Padstow greeted him with a smile.

'Your friend has been in asking after you.'

'Dinkworthy?'

'Neither Mrs Potts nor I gave you away. However, he didn't seem to believe us. In fact, I think we're under suspicion ourselves.'

'That figures. Have anything to do with George Mado and your career's at risk.'

'And the Ambassador would like to see you.'

A few minutes later, so far as the British Embassy was concerned, Mado was on his way back to London. As Padstow confirmed there had been a telegram from Stevens authorizing his return to the UK as a matter of urgency. Reading between the lines, Mado realized that they actively wanted him out of it now. With the Russian invasion of Czechoslovakia, the whole scene had changed.

He imagined the Powder Train operation had either been started too soon and gone off at half-cock or had been cancelled. At any rate, so far as he could judge, it was no longer one of London's top priorities. He wondered how Corby and Dinkworthy would set about keeping him quiet – but then without proof, what danger were they in?

'You'll need an exit visa,' Padstow said, taking his British passport, 'and I don't think you should apply for it in person, do you, sport?'

'I think we should go into business together,' Mado said.

'I thought we already were,' Padstow said, giving the passport to Mrs Potts with a nod. When she had left the room, he passed Mado a slip of paper. 'That's my father's friend in the Household,' he said, 'and that's his ex-directory telephone number.'

Mado memorized the name and the number and then screwed up the piece of paper into a ball.

'Thanks,' he said, throwing it into the wastepaper basket, 'I'll just file it away.'

At that moment Dinkworthy came into the room. He was evidently under strain but still managed a show of nonchalance.

'Ah! there you are, Mado,' he said, 'I wondered when you'd show up.' Then before Mado had time to reply, he went on quickly to Padstow, 'We have another situation on our hands – and a somewhat urgent one at that. Elissa Tarnham and her two children are downstairs in the waiting-room. She's left Tarnham and wants us to get her back to England as soon as we can. She has no luggage, no papers – nothing – and she doesn't dare return to the flat. She says Tarnham's gone – presumably to Russia – and there was an attempt on their lives last night.'

The Ambassador decided that they 'could damn well chaperone each other'. He wanted to get rid of the problem as soon as he could. No scheduled aircraft were flying and so an official car was authorized and Elissa Tarnham, her two children Mark and Lucy, together with Mado set off for the Austrian border in the early afternoon.

Mado had never met Tarnham's wife before, although the Press attention given to the famous defection had made Elissa's features internationally known. She was a lithe, attractive woman with high cheekbones, which reminded him of Anna, grey-green eyes and good teeth. She had a hard expression and a restless movement of the eyes and mouth which Mado recognized as a sign of extreme tension. The children looked stunned and defeated, listlessly watching the countryside go past and not saying a word. Poor little bastards, Mado thought, what had they done to deserve treatment like this?

To begin with they sat in silence, each immersed in private worries and thoughts. The look on Anna's face as she had left the table last night kept bobbing up in Mado's mind like a buoy in a stormy sea. He had never seen her so palsied with fear and this was odd, when he came to think of it, since she had grown up under Communism and must therefore be fully alive to the fear syndrome.

Physically she was so staunch and her body so wonderfully and amply satisfying that he had come to look on her as a rock in every respect. The events of the previous night had shown her to be far more frail than he had imagined. He knew now that he loved her and needed her to a degree he had never experienced. He knew now that this was the object he had to achieve, even if he risked his life in the attempt.

Yet behind it all the possibility that she had consciously acted as a decoy in taking him to the mill nagged away at him as he tried to marshal his thoughts. What was he doing sitting in this car being shipped off to the West, when Anna had been abducted to Russia as he had himself so short a time ago? What was it best to do? What could he do? He turned and looked at Elissa Tarnham.

'You must be in a state of utter chaos and confusion,' he said to break the silence.

'Yes, I am.'

'That makes two of us,' Mado said.

'Are we going to have any trouble at the border, do you think?'

Mado shrugged his shoulders. A silence followed. Then the boy turned round and looked at him.

'You were the one who nearly broke my father's jaw, weren't you?'

'Yes, Mark. I'm sorry it was your father.'

'Everyone says that,' the boy said simply and then, a little later, 'They tried to shoot us from across the street. Father had just gone out and then there were these shots through the window.' His matter-of-fact, ten-year-old voice made it sound so appallingly casual that Mado felt a surge of emotion in his heart.

'So they could have been trying for your husband,' he said to Elissa.

'They could have but they weren't. They just wanted us out of the way.'

'They shot my teddy,' Lucy said, beginning to cry. 'One of the bullets went through my teddy's ear.'

Elissa comforted the child and they relapsed into silence again.

'Have you any idea – any plans as to what to do when you get back?' he asked a little later on. She shook her head.

'Survive, I suppose. I was too young for the war but I suppose being a refugee in one's own country is a timeless experience.'

'Which is your country?' Mado said coolly but not unkindly. She had good, steady eyes and a sort of wiriness he supposed some men would find attractive. That and a granite hardness underneath. It seemed a terrible waste.

'I don't think it matters any more when you've made the mistakes I seem to have made.'

'Don't all of us?' Mado said. 'And if you want a cliché for the trip – isn't that what life is about?' He paused and then added: 'Perhaps your Greek friend will help you again.'

'I'm not sure my Greek friend wasn't behind the shooting this morning,' Elissa said, staring out into the distance. 'I'm pretty sure he had Rupert Eynsham killed.'

'I thought Eynsham committed suicide.'

She looked at him in the way a cat will sometimes study a child.

'Didn't they put it about that you went back to Russia of your own accord?'

'I'm going there now,' Mado said, out of the blue. 'I'll take you as far as Vienna and then you're on your own.'

She considered this for a second or two.

'You must really be mad,' she said.

'Thank you,' Mado said, 'it seems to be a generally held opinion.'

16

The Czechs were still in charge of the frontier, even though Ivan was watching. They crossed into the freedom of Austria without trouble or delay, the first time since Beirut that Mado had not turned round instinctively to see if he was being followed.

Elissa, too, seemed to relax and by the time they reached Vienna, had regained what Mado took to be her normal composure. Whilst sympathizing with the plight she and the children were in, he did not warm to Elissa. He could not comprehend any woman marrying Paul Tarnham, and although he realized that this was basically an emotional reaction, the Tarnhams – man and wife – represented in his mind a matchless example of the 'Philby flaw' in British security. This was the reliance on the old-boy network which was, in fact, veined with hypocrisy but which kept its key importance simply because the Establishment would never accept that men of Tarnham's class could possibly be disloyal.

Paul Tarnham had always been the real enemy – though exactly of what he could not define. Elissa Tarnham was now a victim of the process, but for how long had she known of her husband's real activities? Studying her covertly in the car, he decided that even if she answered a direct question of this kind, he could never trust her to be telling the truth. In reality he did not take to her at all. He was sorry for the children but he had come to the conclusion that Elissa was not quite as innocent as she would like it thought.

It was evening when they reached the British Embassy in Vienna.

'You have an hour to get to the airport,' the Duty Officer

told them, giving them their tickets. 'You have seats on a BEA flight to Zürich, where you will be wait-listed for onward passage to London.'

When they reached Schwechat Airport, Elissa said to him quietly:

'You didn't mean what you said in the car, did you? You are coming on to London with us, aren't you?'

'I almost never mean what I say, especially to strange ladies in cars.'

'I'm not all that strange,' Elissa said, 'and it would certainly be of great help to us if you did.'

He wondered casually if there was another invitation implicit in this and then put the notion firmly away.

'I'm just going to get some cigarettes,' he said, as they queued up for passport control. Then before she had time to reply, he slipped quickly away round a corner and along to the Aeroflot desk. Three hours later he was in Warsaw and, four hours after that, as dawn broke, he stepped down on to the tarmac at Sheremetievo Airport, Moscow. The *laissez-passer* given him by General Simonov was certainly highly effective.

Now that it was too late to turn back, the personal panic began. Now he was quite alone. His guts seemed to be melting as he walked from the aircraft to the terminal building in the cool Moscow morning. This was undoubtedly the most idiotic action he had ever taken in his life – a futile quixotic gesture which would impress no one, achieve nothing and simply result in a further and possibly final disposal of himself to prison.

As he reached the terminal building, he turned and looked back at the aircraft, much as a lone sailor takes his last look at land before it disappears below the horizon.

'You English are crazy,' a voice said as he turned his back on the aircraft. 'Why have you come to Moscow at this time?'

It was General Simonov. He was in uniform and alone.

'You gave me this,' Mado said, showing his *laissez-passer*. 'I was sure you meant me to use it.'

'You have come for your girl, haven't you?'

'For my girl, for my son and for that little black book you showed me in your office.'

Simonov laughed. The incongruity of being met at dawn by a general in the KGB who actually laughed, threw Mado off balance. He had not expected this nor to discover in the process that the man might be human.

'I was sure you understood Russian better than you pretended,' Simonov said, leading him with a curt gesture of authority away from the ordinary passport control, through the building and out to a waiting car.

'In the car you talk in English,' Simonov said. 'You talk generally about the list of foreign correspondents in Prague which you have brought and who need to be watched – and the weather, of course, since you are English.'

The driver saluted and held open the door. On the way into Moscow, Simonov said:

'You'd like some Russian tea, I expect,' and without waiting for Mado to answer gave the driver a sharp order. A few moments later they were sitting in a busy café surrounded by factory workers.

'We are very democratic here,' Simonov said. 'Here we can talk. Now tell me why you are really here.'

'For you,' Mado said, taking a risk.

'How do you mean – for me? You're not seriously expecting me to come with you to London, are you? If you want my opinion I much doubt you will ever see London again yourself. I wouldn't take a bet on it.'

'Who knows the mind of Allah?'

Again Simonov laughed and again Mado found this disconcerting without knowing why.

'The reports on you were right. You really do have nerve.'

Mado shrugged his shoulders.

'I've been within sight of losing my life a number of times.'

'You are now.'

'But possibly I'm not alone – and there must be some reason why you gave me that special passport and why you, a great general in the KGB come to the airport at this time of the morning to meet someone who could be put away with a flick of the eyes. Perhaps I can be of help to you. Perhaps we can do a deal. Perhaps there is something you want from me – some personal help I can give?'

'What do you think you can offer that could possibly equal what you want?'

'Let's keep it in proportion,' Mado said. 'The lives of two young people don't matter all that much to Russia, do they? Say the word and hurry them away.'

'Your son and his friends are guilty of distributing anti-Soviet propaganda and will no doubt go to prison for their schoolboy pranks.'

'That's the first I knew of it. I don't suppose the evidence was planted on them, was it?'

General Simonov ignored the sarcasm.

'The girl is a hostage for her father. Who knows what her fate will be? Now tell me what you have to offer?'

Mado paused a moment and glanced round. The General had chosen well. The place was crowded, noisy and disinterested in them. He leant forward.

'You were with Oleg Penkovsky at the Second Artillery School at Kiev, weren't you?'

'The traitor Penkovsky – yes.'

Both men examined each other minutely. In the end, Mado thought, it's all just a game of poker. You have to judge, guess and then gamble.

'A traitor to what?' Mado said. 'Penkovsky saved humanity from a possible nuclear war.'

The General looked at him in silence. This was the point of decision. From here on there would be no going back. Neither spoke for what seemed to be a considerable time. Then at last the General said quietly:

'I agree. You are as shrewd as I thought. You have put your finger on it, my friend, at very great risk to yourself. Now I will commit myself as well. The madmen must be contained: somehow or other the madmen must be kept under control.'

'We have madmen, too,' Mado said, 'and their form of madness is to destroy the balance which others give their lives to achieve. Like Paul Tarnham. Like Sir Graham Corby.' The General nodded slightly. 'Like Simon Dinkworthy.' To this there was no response. Again followed a steady look and a long pause.

'So you have nothing to offer,' Simonov said in the end, 'but have only come to ask.'

'Not at all,' Mado countered. 'Here in Moscow my life – our lives – are in your hands. In London I can offer you access – direct access – to the highest in the land. If only you will come.'

Now that he had played his hand, he waited to see how the General would react. Predictably the Russian mentality went off at a tangent.

'The Aeroflot message announcing your arrival will go to other people,' Simonov said. 'I can only protect you for a certain time. That is why I originally sent you to Prague.'

'I haven't come here for protection.'

'I dare say not but you're going to need it.'

'I've come for you,' Mado said again, 'and for my girl – as you said – and for my son.'

'I respect your courage.'

'Thank you.'

'You say you have access to the highest in the land? You seriously mean the Queen of England?'

'Penkovsky saw her,' Mado said, 'and that was possibly because of pride – or vanity, if you like.'

'And what would it be for me?'

'I don't know,' Mado said, 'but for us it would be to do with the safety of the realm ... and there wouldn't be much point in taking you to Sir Graham Corby, would there?'

'That proves it to my mind,' Dinkworthy said. 'That's the second time he's gone to Russia of his own accord. If he were anything other than what we know him to be, that would mean prison or death or both in that order. So they must be really looking after him. He must be in their pay, as we always suspected he might be in Beirut.'

The Chief gave the problem a moment's attention, thinking what a fool Dinkworthy was. They were in one of their rare meetings in the Cabinet Offices and Sir Graham had just reported to the Prime Minister.

'I've told the PM about Tarnham and Mado. I suppose we'd better grab him back willy nilly.'

The Chief looked as if his mind was on other things.

'Mrs Tarnham's still under interrogation,' Dinkworthy said. 'Her reunion with Tarnham doesn't seem to have been significant for any reasons which would interest us. I mean even now she doesn't seem to realize what he was really doing – nor for whom.'

'She says her impression of Mado in the short time they were together was of a man obsessed. Of course it's the girl he's after, isn't it? That fatal weakness for young girls.'

'You forget they're also holding his son,' Sir Graham said, giving Dinkworthy one of his 'God what a bore you are!' looks. How had he ever let Dinkworthy get where he was?

'I don't think he gives a damn for the boy. And certainly the boy doesn't for him. The only thing I don't understand is why Mado attacked Tarnham in Marides' room. I mean if they're really working together.'

'The *only* thing you don't understand?' the Chief said testily. 'Really, Simon, there are times when you not only play thick – you *are* thick.'

'Thank you, sir.' Dinkworthy put on his 'water-off-aduck's-back' smile which always infuriated the Chief.

'Anyway, get Mado back or get him silenced. He knows far too much for everyone's good, your own included.'

'Stevens is sending Shelton to Moscow on the afternoon plane. But which faction is now on top in the Kremlin – the hawks or the doves?'

As usual Sir Graham avoided answering direct questions by asking one of his own.

'Do you imagine there are really going to be any doves in Russia now that they've invaded Czechoslovakia? All our calculations have to be rethought since August 21st.'

Dinkworthy shrugged his shoulders. The Chief was clearly in one of his difficult moods.

'It strikes me as a great waste of everyone's efforts to abandon Powder Train at a crucial time like this.'

'Then you'd better tell the Prime Minister yourself. You know how he relishes criticism.'

Dinkworthy gave the Chief one of his hurt-spaniel looks. It was definitely a 'non-speakers' day.

'I think we should have made Paul Tarnham a more generous offer. We could certainly use him now.'

'Does it not occur to you that that's been taken care of?' the Chief said acidly. 'I sometimes ask myself if you have the first idea of what it's all about.'

Suddenly Dinkworthy had had enough.

'I have a perfectly clear idea of what it's all about – and so have you. We both of us know the risks involved.'

This was open rebellion of a dangerous kind. The Chief gave him one of his icy, penetrating looks which had always, up to now, protected him more effectively than armour-plating. Dinkworthy had never been as outright as this before. Then he said quietly:

'Are you speaking personally, Simon?'

'I think that's a rhetorical question,' Dinkworthy said, with equal frigidity. 'We both of us know our respective roles in this matter – and what is at stake. I think I'd better go with Shelton this afternoon.'

'Yes,' said Sir Graham. 'In view of the situation, I think perhaps you should.'

After they had finished their Russian tea, General Simonov took Mado back to his office in the Kremlin. It was again an extraordinary experience to walk into the holy of holies without let or hindrance – even stranger to Mado than when he had previously left it in Simonov's company. Under surveillance though they undoubtedly were, no sentry, no official, no minion of any kind asked for a pass, stopped or checked them in any way. As a small demonstration of power, Mado could think of nothing more calculated to impress.

'After our discussion,' Simonov said while they traversed the endless corridors, 'I shall send you to an address where you will stay until we decide what is to be done. You realize, of course, that you are not exactly alone in these circumstances in Russia today. You are English but there are French, German, Swedish, even American George Mados in Moscow—'

'As there are General Simonovs in London, Paris and New York.'

'No. There is only one General Simonov.'

Mado studied this extraordinary man who had taken him on trust and who was forced to communicate all the time in a double talk not always interpretable. As they penetrated farther into the Kremlin, the sense of doom and oppression filled his heart in spite of a conscious effort to ward it off.

'I am glad you are seeing things our way at last,' the General said in a loud voice as they entered his office. Even in General Simonov's high position, it was evidently still necessary to play to the micro. Simonov walked round his desk, indicating that Mado should take a seat. Then pressing a button on the left side of the desk, he nodded briskly to a man who appeared from a door to an inner office, and a few moments later Anna came into the room, at first sight rigid with fear. Then, seeing Mado, she gave a gasp of delight and flew into his arms, watched by General Simonov with a sardonic smile.

'You see, Mr Mado,' he said, 'we are not monsters after all.'

'Are you all right?' Mado asked and she shook her head buried in his shoulder, clinging to him as if she were on the point of drowning.

'However,' Simonov continued, 'we are not running a reunion service for foreigners here. Since you have both come as representatives of the Czechoslovak Student Organizations to request our help in defending your movement against the counter-revolutionaries who are threatening the whole fabric of socialism in your unhappy country – we must see what can now be done.'

As when he had first sat in this office, it was obvious to Mado that the General was adept at feeding into the listening devices the sort of material it or they wanted to hear.

'You have taken a risk in acting as you have done but we shall see you are given the support you need in your struggle against imperialist aggression. I will arrange a meeting later today with others who can be of practical help.' The trite platform phrases came out as if the General were addressing some dreary fraternal meeting, but he was smiling at them both in an almost kindly fashion which thus made even more nonsense of the actual words which came out of his mouth.

Mado had always been deeply inspired by the courage of those few who face up to their dangerous fate alone and without support. Now, watching this latter-day Penkovsky with a decision which must in reality have been taken some time ago – in mid-stream with a course of action which could prove to be suddenly fateful at any point – he realized that real communication in their present circumstances could only take place through the eyes. The truth was there in the eyes. There were no words for what the eyes were so clearly expressing.

The character of Pontius Pilate had always been a

fascinating enigma to Mado, who was not a conventionally religious man, and watching the General now it came to him that the central question on which the whole Christian faith depended must have been answered then as now without words but with the eyes, when Pilate had had Jesus brought close and had asked him, as man to man, 'But are you the Son of God?' The answer was in the eyes.

A telephone gave a single, quiet buzz and the General picked it up, said 'Yes', and listened. It was a fairly short communication, during which the General said 'Yes' twice more in an authoritative way and then put down the phone.

'I can give you no more of my time at present,' he said, 'but I will see you later in the day.'

He then addressed himself to Anna, indicating with a brief gesture that she should separate herself from Mado.

'You will be pleased to hear that your father has arrived in Moscow and has agreed to cooperate with the liberating forces in securing a normalization of strict socialist principle in Czechoslovakia. I am arranging for you to join him now.'

He summoned an aide and gave a series of sharp orders. Mado could see that Anna was still desperately afraid and the shivering had returned. She evidently did not believe what she had just been told and, giving him a stricken look, was led out through one of the inner doors.

'Come on, sport, try for a smile. I did come back to get you,' Mado said and was pleased to receive a tiny answering flicker before the door closed after her. He wondered what they had done to break her down to such an extent.

When they were for a moment alone, the General said:

'You I am sending to the British Embassy, who may be somewhat surprised to receive you,' and then to Mado's complete astonishment he gave him the little black book from the top right-hand drawer of his desk. 'I have to go back to Prague tomorrow and it may be necessary for you to come too, but we will meet again this evening. Be at this address at seven o'clock.' He quickly wrote down an address and passed it across. Then he buzzed for another assistant, to whom he gave the necessary orders. As Mado left, the General picked up the phone and said:

'All right, I'll see Marides now.'

17

So what about that then? Mado said chirpily to himself as the KGB car sped him to the British Embassy. How about that for a lark? There was now no going back so far as General Simonov was concerned. He was totally committed in this totally unpredictable way. Feeling the pressure of the little black book in his pocket, Mado wondered what had impelled the General to this dangerous and irrevocable act. What was really going on unseen in the background which would drive a man of Simonov's calibre to this possibly suicidal and certainly treasonable behaviour? Perhaps Sir Graham Corby had been right and the hawks were attacking the doves in such a way that a dangerous upheaval in the Kremlin had already begun. Perhaps another kind of powder train had already been lit, burning its way into the central magazine.

However, that sort of question could wait. Now that he had Penkovsky the second in his own personal one-man act, there was some urgent work to be done. If the little black book revealed what he was certain it would, he had the task of getting Simonov and himself back to England without Corby, Dinkworthy or any of their lower echelons discovering what had happened. Padstow had been right after all. He must take this highly valuable, highly volatile, living evidence to the very top, by-passing the minefield of higher officials in the British Security Service whose own careers would be suddenly at stake and whose interest it would therefore be to prevent General Simonov from spilling the beans.

The General had certainly been correct in one statement he had made. The British Embassy was astonished and none too pleased to see Mado. He was taken in for a brief interview with a senior Embassy official, where he was coolly received.

'We knew you had made your own way back to Moscow, Mr Mado, but I hardly expected you to seek asylum as quickly as this.'

'I haven't asked for asylum.'

'Then what is it you want? The Foreign Office are sending someone out to cope with you this afternoon.'

'Very considerate of them,' Mado said with his tongue in his cheek, 'but I don't need to be coped with. I simply want my son out of Russia as quickly as possible.'

'I'm afraid there are other somewhat more important things on hand at the moment.'

'Not to me there aren't.' He felt like letting himself go but stopped in time. There was no point in being needlessly aggressive when it was the Embassy's help he wanted. 'I'm sorry if I've offended against protocol in some way but—'

'I would scarcely call it protocol, Mr Mado. In any case Mr Shelton will be dealing with you when he arrives, whether you like it or not.'

'I may not be here.'

'I think you will be,' the official said brusquely and indicated that the interview was at an end.

It had not occurred to him that he would be virtually a prisoner in his own country's Embassy, but as he thought out the implications, he realized that this may have been exactly what General Simonov intended. He had disposed of some vital evidence and its carrier in one swift move. Both had been placed, at least temporarily, out of KGB control, and aided by his London contacts the reason could be to keep Mado out of the current Kremlin field of play.

Perhaps the General had no intention of keeping the seven o'clock appointment he had set up. It was possible that Mado had read him wrongly. The Penkovksy syndrome might not be what it was all about. It struck him that he had clearly been meant to hear that the next visitor was Marides. Yet if this were really so why had he been given the little black book? He badly needed a Padstow whom he could trust and whom he could use as a sounding board. In the event he was aware of a cool but considerable antipathy in the Embassy staff, and especially from Henderson, the Padstow equivalent, with whom he had mostly to deal.

The next extraordinary happening to startle the afternoon calm of the British Embassy in Moscow was the arrival of Brewster MacFish and the entire Wanderlust pop group, including Philip Carlton. They had been held in a so-called 'accommodation centre' some fifty miles outside Moscow and were in sorry shape, though no physical damage had been done to any of them.

None of them knew why they had suddenly been released except that it had been on General Simonov's orders. They had simply been told to be ready in ten minutes' time and had then been transported to Moscow in a lorry and dumped at the Embassy. A little later some coloured students from one of the emergent countries also appeared. Their own Embassy, it transpired, was closed for a public holiday. Things were hotting up.

By the time Shelton and Dinkworthy arrived in Moscow, Mado had examined and memorized the contents of the little black book. He did this in the lavatory so that no one even knew that he had it in his possession, and he then continued to keep it hidden. It was a shattering document.

Beginning with Sir Graham Corby, it contained the names of key people at every level, so far as Mado could tell, in British diplomatic and security life, including Shelton, the Foreign Office troubleshooter, and three of the people who had seen him that day at the Embassy. Oddly enough Dinkworthy's name was not in the book, an omission which Mado found inexplicable.

The disturbing thing was that there seemed to be two

or three people in every sensitive area, each with a specialist job and each of whom could be called upon for different services. If he could get this book and Simonov himself to England, the effect on Whitehall would be catastrophic. The Simonov net would be the black scandal of the century, so far as the British Establishment was concerned. It made Philby look like a young Conservative.

Shelton was a brisk, hard, humourless man. Dinkworthy had had to do with him on two previous occasions but had never before accompanied him on an inquisitorial mission. Shelton, he discovered, had come some way from his wartime experience as a sergeant in the Intelligence Corps. He was now, perhaps, the best interrogator in the business.

He was also the sort of man whose company Dinkworthy least enjoyed. It was regrettable, Dinkworthy told himself, that he should have allowed himself to be stung by anger and the Chief into coming on this trip at all.

'My brief is simply to search Mado out, discover what he has to tell and bring him back with me to England, which from Russia may be difficult and take a little time,' he had told Dinkworthy on the plane. Dinkworthy personally thought it impossible but kept his opinion to himself. It was not until they reached the Embassy that they were told the incredible news that no searching out was necessary, that Mado had walked into the Embassy that morning and was now safely in British hands.

'He showed signs of treating us as an hotel,' the Ambassador told them, 'but it was made clear that as you were coming out especially to deal with him, he must stick around in the Embassy until you arrived. So he's all yours and the sooner you can get him out of my parish the happier I shall be. Henderson knows the drill for exit visas and that side of things. Take him away and never let me see him again.'

The Ambassador rang for his secretary and summoned

Henderson, who appeared almost instantly, white-faced and clearly in a state of shock.

'I'm afraid Mado's gone, sir,' he said. 'He took a car authorization form from my desk, forged your signature and has gone off in one of the cars from the pool. The driver was a little surprised but as it was your signature, he didn't check back. I'm terribly sorry, only I don't see what I can do.'

Outside Shelton said:

'I'll tell you what you can do, laddie. Forge the Ambassador's signature yourself, draw a gun from the armoury and shoot yourself. It's going to be the easier way out.'

The address Mado had been given turned out to be a small apartment in one of the older blocks. The door was opened by a young woman with a baby in her arms, who looked as if she had been crying.

'Come in,' she said, 'I know all about you. I am Tanya Simonov. My father will be back in half an hour. He was called unexpectedly to a meeting.'

There was no one else in the apartment and when she had put the baby back in its cot, she came over and sat down beside him. She had started to cry again.

'Is there anything I can do?' Mado asked gently.

'There is nothing anyone can do. I know my father. Once his mind is made up, he will never change.'

'Can we talk?' Mado said, giving a quick glance round the room to see where the listening devices were likely to be. She nodded miserably.

'It no longer matters,' she said. 'They will simply send us away or kill us all.'

'Where is your husband?'

'In Leningrad. He will not be back till next week. And that will be much too late.'

In the next few minutes Mado pieced together the missing parts of the story. There was indeed a power struggle in progress in the Kremlin, in which General Simonov was deeply concerned. He had opposed the invasion of Czechoslovakia. He thought Brezhnev an evil and dangerous man.

'If only my mother were alive,' Tanya said, 'it might have been different. She could have calmed him down. But I am all he has now. My father is a man of integrity and of strong, passionate feeling. He is disgusted by what he knows goes on in the Central Committee. You may not think – you English – that a man can be a general in the KGB and keep his integrity. My father has up to now. We have honourable men in Russia,' she said with the tears starting from her eyes.

'But what decided him to go?'

She looked at him without speaking for a time.

'It may well have been you.'

'I don't see how that can possibly be so.'

'You,' she said with the same low ferocity which Anna had in her voice. 'You – and what he calls your guts in coming back. He admires the English very much – the people that is, not their politics. He is a good Communist not a capitalist under the skin, but he still admires you English for your integrity and loyalty and . . .' she paused for the words, 'and for generally being everything that Paul Tarnham isn't. He hates that sort of man.'

'But he is dealing with treachery every day of his life. It's his business – his stock in trade, if you like.'

'I know my father,' she said simply, 'and he has had enough. He has a contempt for the men who are running Russia today. He says there will be another Stalin in a matter of months – when a few more people have been got out of the way – including himself. And he is also disgusted that the English are being sold to us every day without their knowledge, behind their backs and by people right at the top – by people they trust. Then you came along.'

'I didn't exactly come of my own accord.'

'No, but he saw how you behaved under stress. He watched you very carefully, as he watched Greville Wynne and other Englishmen who were brought up free and then subjected to ...' she waved vaguely in a hopeless fashion, 'to the slavery here.'

'Individuals are all different,' Mado said gently.

'Then you had the courage to come back for your girl and your son. My father admires courage. He told me you are as reckless as a Russian – and that's a compliment. That's why he arranged for Anna Novaček to be released and sent back today, that's why your son's at the British Embassy – he did this for you. He is taking you to Prague tomorrow and from there on it is up to you. He is relying on you to take him straight to the top. Otherwise he is lost – and so are you. He knows too much and now you are also fully involved.'

'But what about you? You said earlier on that you are all he has left.'

'Naturally he wants me to come as well. He still has the power to arrange these things. He is very near the top. He can still do almost anything he likes. But I have a husband and a child. My life is with them.'

'Wouldn't your husband—?' Mado began but she shook her head.

'My husband's father is a Stalinist of the old school in the Central Committee. And my husband agrees with him. My father and my husband do not see eye to eye.'

'Perhaps that will protect you then.'

She shrugged her shoulders and looked over to the baby in the cot.

'Do you ever hear of Penkovsky's family these days? We shall simply disappear.' The tears began again. Mado took her hand and held it in his. She was warm and attractive, not especially pretty but young and alive. He felt very moved. He thought how much of his life had been spent in the pursuit and the pleasing of very young women. This is what it's all about, Alfie, he said to himself. All that wasted time and effort, as so many people had told him with contempt, just to end up holding a young woman's hand – a young woman he had only met a few minutes before and whom he would probably never see again, a young woman in an alien land, living through her own agonizing crisis and trying somehow or other to find the strength and the courage she was soon so obviously going to need.

At that moment the General came in. He appeared distraught and at once Mado sensed that something must have gone very wrong. There was a surge of danger in the air. He nodded curtly at Mado and said to his daughter:

'We are going now. All of us. There is a plane being held for us now. Tomorrow will be too late. Take your baby and come as you are. Now.'

She shook her head and rushed into his arms.

'I can't. I can't. You know I can't.'

'The car is waiting. We must go at once.'

'Why? What has happened?'

'There's no time to explain. Simply take the baby and come.'

'No,' she said and drew away, 'I am staying here.'

They looked at each other for what seemed to Mado an aeon of time. Then in a great burst of sobbing she rushed once more into her father's arms, clinging to him in the way that Anna had clung to Mado that morning in Simonov's office. It occurred to Mado that the General, who was himself showing signs of nervous collapse, might be trapped by this Russian orgy of emotion into leaving it all too late.

However, she broke free, turned her back and then threw herself down on the sofa in a fresh gush of tears. By this time the baby was caterwauling from its cot and it was in this tempest of sound and feeling that they left. The General walked out of the apartment without looking back and without saying another word. Mado followed, closing the door afterwards with the desperate feeling that this was the end of a life.

Out in the street Mado said, 'I have a British Embassy car. Why don't you send yours on in front and we'll follow behind? In case of one of those accidents ...'

'No,' said the General, 'it is not as bad as that but tomorrow a great deal more will be known – thanks to Sir Graham Corby and the man he sent out to interrogate you today. So I decided to go at once. I have legitimate business in Prague. Once we are there the immediate problems will be different.'

They drove to the airport at such speed that even Mado was scared. But there were no delays. No hindrances were put in their way. Time might be running out but the General in his car, like the General walking into the Kremlin that morning, still carried all imperiously before him. They spoke very little, each being immersed in private thoughts.

Mado wondered if Anna had yet got back to Prague and when he would see her again – but he did not let himself dream for long, there were too many practical problems lying immediately ahead.

At the airport itself the car was evidently expected. One of the General's subordinates slipped in with the driver and directed them out on to the tarmac to a military aircraft which started its engines as the car approached. The aircraft itself was only half-full, with a mixture of civilians and military, and as soon as they were aboard it began to taxi out to the runway.

The General indicated with a gesture that they should sit apart on opposite sides of the aisle, so that they were not obviously together. In a few more moments, Mado said to himself, it would be goodbye to Russia for ever. He glanced over at the General, who seemed to have gone very pale. He felt a sudden compassion for the man in the turmoil of emotion he must surely be suffering. As the aircraft began to near the runway for the take-off, Mado braced himself for the last few moments when the danger would be greatest of all.

They had only gone a few yards when suddenly the engines cut and the plane braked quickly to a halt. A few moments later the pilot came through and spoke to

General Simonov, who got up looking whiter than ever, and without a glance at Mado walked to the rear of the aircraft. In the sudden silence a car could be heard approaching at speed and a little later it drew up at the aircraft door, which had now been opened.

The other passengers in the plane had turned round to watch, so Mado could take a quick look without attracting attention to himself. Two huge uniformed soldiers appeared, saluted and gave the General a slip of paper, which he read with a frown. Then again, without looking at Mado, he climbed down the ladder and was gone.

The pilot returned to the controls, Mado heard the door slam shut and then the engines were restarted. He wondered if the aircraft would return to the apron but it was evidently intended now to continue with the flight, although this he only believed when they were actually in the air and rapidly gaining height.

It was only then that a man came from the rear of the aircraft and sat down in the seat next to Mado.

'I'm sorry General Simonov was so abruptly recalled,' said Jean-Pierre Mournier or Karel Zilina or whoever he really was, 'but as you and I have a little unfinished business to discuss, I'm sure you won't mind me taking his place.'

Mado studied the dark, sardonic features of the killer who had first come into his life so many aeons ago in Beirut. Mournier reminded him of the sort of Mafia man you saw in the big gambling clubs of London.

'I can scarcely get out of the aircraft now.'

'That's right,' Mournier said, producing a small automatic and pointing it at Mado's crutch. 'It gives us a little time to straighten things out.'

'If you use that gun now you'll destroy the aircraft.'

'Possibly, but if I were you I wouldn't gamble on it. However, I'm quite sure that it won't be necessary to use force, Mr Mado. You are far too intelligent and experienced a man. This is just to remind you of the realities of the situation.'

'Great!' Mado said. 'You've made your point. So put it away.'

Surprisingly Mournier slipped the gun into his pocket and smiled.

'I don't think you'll be running out on us a second time,' he said. There was a short, high-tension pause.

'Now I believe General Simonov had a small black book of very interesting names,' Mournier went on, 'and as I don't think the General will be leaving Russia again, I feel reasonably sure we can come to terms.'

'What did you have in mind?'

The incongruity of Mournier's conversational tone would have made Mado laugh if only he could have controlled the panic tingling in his bladder. Instinctively he knew the game was up. He had finally failed. Equally his gambler's instinct drove him to continue to the very end.

'The little black book, of course. Mr Marides is awaiting it in Prague.'

Mado risked a last desperate bluff.

'You don't think I'm stupid enough to carry it with me, do you? I left it in the British Embassy in Moscow.'

'Oh! no you didn't. You have it in your left-hand trouser pocket.'

Mado held the pause for as long as he dared and then with a feeling of sickening abandonment and despair reached into his pocket and handed over the book. Mournier flipped casually through its pages and then slipped it into his breast pocket. There was a look almost of disappointment on his face.

'Good,' he said with a grim, tight little smile. 'You just saved your life – for the present, that is.'

'I believe you,' Mado said sincerely. 'What happens now?'

The other shrugged his shoulders and looked out of the window at the night sky. There was another almost endless pause.

'Mr Marides and the Russians have this in common,'

Mournier said eventually. 'They have the power and the money to pay for the things they want. The question for you is a simple one. Does anyone want your services any more? What have you left to offer?'

Then with a curt nod he got up and returned to his seat at the rear of the aircraft. Below the Carpathian mountains, invisible in the darkness of the night, caused the aircraft to bump suddenly in the turbulence.

Mado looked out at the blackness as the aircraft droned on its way. The manner in which Mournier had dealt with him and the question he had left him with struck him merely as an exercise in macabre humour. He now had no cards left in his hand. Mournier knew this and Mado knew that he knew. True, his life had been spared but presumably this was because now that Marides had got what he wanted, it would be more troublesome to kill him off in the present circumstances than simply to allow him to disappear from the scene as best he could – if he could.

He smiled grimly to himself. 'Does anyone want your services any more?' and 'What have you left to offer?' He lit a cigarette and wished he could lay his hands on a drink. The short answer to both questions was a simple and resounding No.

Warren Tute

'A thoroughly professional writer. His characters are neatly introduced and described. His dialogue, like his plot, is crisp and convincing.' ARGOSY MAGAZINE

THE ROCK 40p

'Holds the attention like a magnetic mine' – WESTERN MAIL

'An absorbing novel of love and war' – EAST ANGLIAN DAILY TIMES

'A remarkable success . . . brilliantly depicted and intensely interesting' – THE TIMES

A MATTER OF DIPLOMACY 25p

'I enjoyed it immensely. It is an altogether admirable invasion into le Carré territory' – C. P. SNOW

'Well worked out, prepossessingly written . . . never for a moment dull' – SUNDAY TIMES

'A most plausible and authentic-sounding novel, one which I heartily recommend' – COVENTRY EVENING TELEGRAPH